NAUGHTY NIGHTS

Other Ellora's Cave Anthologies Available from Pocket Books

MIDNIGHT TREAT
by Sally Painter, Maragaret L. Carter, & Shelley Munro

ROYAL BONDAGE
by Samantha Winston, Delilah Devlin, & Marianne LaCroix

MAGICAL SEDUCTION
by Cathryn Fox, Mandy M. Roth, & Anya Bast

GOOD GIRL SEEKS BAD RIDER
by Vonna Harper, Lena Matthews, & Ruth D. Kerce

ROAD TRIP TO PASSION
by Sahara Kelly, Lani Aames, & Vonna Harper

OVERTIME, UNDER HIM
by N. J. Walters, Susie Charles, & Jan Springer

GETTING WHAT SHE WANTS
by Diana Hinter, S. L. Carpenter, & Chris Tanglen

INSATIABLE
by Sherri L. King, Elizabeth Jewell, & S. L. Carpenter

HIS FANTASIES, HER DREAMS
by Sherri L. King, S. L. Carpenter, & Trista Ann Michaels

MASTER OF SECRET DESIRES
by S. L. Carpenter, Elizabeth Jewell, & Tawny Taylor

BEDTIME, PLAYTIME
by Jaid Black, Sherri L. King, & Ruth D. Kerce

HURTS SO GOOD
by Gail Faulkner, Lisa Renee Jones, & Sahara Kelly

LOVER FROM ANOTHER WORLD
by Rachel Carrington, Elizabeth Jewell, & Shiloh Walker

FEVER-HOT DREAMS
by Sherri L. King, Jaci Burton, & Samantha Winston

TAMING HIM
by Kimberly Dean, Summer Devon, & Michelle M. Pillow

ALL SHE WANTS
by Jaid Black, Dominique Adair, & Shiloh Walker

NAUGHTY NIGHTS

CHARLENE TEGLIA

TAWNY TAYLOR

DAWN RYDER

POCKET BOOKS

NEW YORK LONDON TORONTO SYDNEY

Pocket Books
A Division of Simon & Schuster, Inc.
1230 Avenue of the Americas
New York, NY 10020

First Pocket Books trade paperback edition July 2008

Designed by Jamie Kerner Scott

Manufactured in the United States of America

10 9 8 7 6 5 4 3 2 1

Library of Congress Cataloging-in-Publication Data

Naughty nights / Charlene Teglia, Tawny Taylor, Dawn Ryder.—1st Pocket Books Trade pbk. ed.
p. cm. — (Ellora's Cave anthologies)
1. Erotic stories, American. I. Teglia, Charlene. II. Taylor, Tawny. III. Ryder, Dawn.

PS648.E7N38 2008
813'.60803538—dc22 2007047664

ISBN-13: 978-1-4165-7729-4
ISBN-10: 1-4165-7729-7

Contents

WOLF IN SHINING ARMOR

Charlene Teglia

Prologue

The Border Lands, 1146

RORIK LOVED THE WOODS. In the night the trees rose black and jagged, forming broken outlines against the starlit sky as they curved overhead in an ancient living canopy above the path he strode. They rustled and murmured with the sounds of hundreds of creatures going about their nocturnal business.

Eerie, to some. To him, it was the sound and sight of home. The Fell Wood outside of Wolf's Keep was rumored to harbor demon wolves who took human form, which served to keep poachers as well as the overly curious far away, and so he found good hunting. This night, aided by the light of the full moon, he followed a line of snares he'd set and baited the day before, checking for game.

His cousin, Simon of Northumberland, accompanied him as always. Somewhat unhappily, Rorik knew. Simon did not quite share either his love of adventure or his appreciation for the Fell Wood at night. As light in heart as he was light of hair, the dark woods held no fascination for him.

Rorik paused to smile at his companion. "Up ahead, I hear something," he said softly. He'd snared a deer, possibly, from the sounds he heard. Something large. Then he frowned as he listened more closely. That wild thrashing did not sound like a deer. He signaled Simon to be quiet and follow closely. At a soft run, he approached the snare and nocked an arrow at the ready.

Then he slowly lowered his bow and replaced the arrow at the sight that met his eyes.

"What are you doing?" Simon hissed, looking agonized. "It is a wolf. A demon wolf, come for our souls. Kill it, quickly."

Rorik waved impatiently at Simon, gesturing for quiet. There were no demons in his woods. This was but a she-wolf caught in a snare meant for other game. A small one, not fully grown. Moonlight touched the black fur, highlighting it with silver and glistening off the glowing eyes. Blood tinged the snow at the beast's feet and tipped the muzzle.

Memory flashed in Rorik's mind, tales of wolf traps found sprung, holding only a forepaw, as the creature fought so fiercely for freedom that it would pay any price. As this wolf would do.

He didn't see danger. Rorik saw only the wolf and felt the injustice, the unbearable horror of its captivity, the panic at running fleet across the snow one moment, inexplicably held prisoner the next.

Rorik slipped slowly up to the snare, holding the wolf's eyes as he did. "Easy," he whispered. "Hush, now." Making his motions careful and steady, he eased one hand to the snare then quickly sprung her loose and stepped back.

Not swiftly enough to evade slashing teeth that tore his chest before the young she-wolf fled into the night.

Simon ran to his aid and staunched the blood with shaking hands. "Rorik? Rorik, do you hear me? Speak," he pleaded.

Rorik stirred and smiled at his companion. "Did you see her, Simon? She was beautiful."

"See what? The wolf?" Simon asked. "I could scarcely miss that."

"No. The girl." Then Rorik fell back, unconscious.

ONE

Fourteen years later . . .

"DO YOU THINK TO find it changed much?" Simon inquired, guiding his gray warhorse beside Rorik's black destrier. The two knights showed the signs of having survived many battles in myriad ways. The armor and equipment showed the lines and dents of hard use, in spite of flawless upkeep, as did the two faces. They were deeply changed, if Wolf's Keep was not, Simon acknowledged.

Rorik didn't answer. Perhaps he had changed most of all, Simon thought. Battle had hardened him. The youthful companion who had risked his life to free a wild wolf had seen too much killing. His moods had grown as dark as his hair and did not seem to be lightening as they neared home.

Known as the Fell Wolf for the bite he'd earned, the rumors that Rorik became a demon wolf had come in useful on many occasions. Absurd, but useful. In the tourneys many an opponent quailed before the black and gray banner, fear and superstition striking more blows than a lance.

As soldiers of fortune, the two had done well. Well enough to permit them to return to Rorik's home, now his by coin as well as birthright, with the full coffers and riches supplied by grateful lords whose lands and holdings they had defended. The earnings would permit them to hold and defend their own land now.

Simon frowned, thinking of that injustice. That Rorik should have to buy back his ancestral home still rankled. But his father's untimely death had allowed an unscrupulous neighboring lord to claim Wolf's Keep, and Rorik had been unable to prevent it, having only fifteen years at the time.

That they were both away, fostered and in training for knighthood at the time, had also forced Rorik to bide his time in reclaiming his home. In his patient way, he'd earned his spurs and set out to make his fortune, first in the tourneys, then as a seasoned soldier for hire, always confident that he would return.

The Fell Wolf was returning now, some ten years later, and Simon nearly pitied Alain Devere. He'd lost the prize he thought to take, and the man could not rest easy of a night, knowing the lord's son was coming home to claim what was his.

Including his betrothed, the lady Elissa Montreade. The shy and lovely girl he recalled had also fostered in Wolf's Keep as Rorik's future bride, the marriage arranged by the old baron shortly after the birth of a daughter to dear friends. She, and no doubt her dowry, had been taken along with the fiefdom by Devere.

He frowned at that thought. They had been in no position to help her sooner, but he did not like to think of the child who had been his youthful shadow under the care of such a man.

Simon eyed his friend once more, thinking Rorik did not look in the least like an eager bridegroom, or a returning hero.

He looked battle-weary and in sore need of a diversion.

"So, Rorik, your hearth and home await, with the lovely lady Elissa soon to grace them both. Will you frighten her with that face of yours?"

Rorik roused himself from his dark thoughts and spared a glance for Simon the chatterer. In truth, it did not feel like a homecoming. Without his parents living, he did not expect to find much of a home waiting. Devere had doubtless let the place fall to ruin under his stewardship. With no lord in residence the able servants had fled, fearing tales of human wolves. Any retainers remaining did so out of blind loyalty or old age.

He did not expect to find much waiting for him. As for his betrothed . . . there he could find something to think on that pleased him. Marriage was a practical business. He did not love Elissa, nor did he expect to. However, enough nights in rough camps made the idea of home and a wife to see to his comfort seem more than adequate compensation for doing his duty.

A wife to make a home from a pile of cold stone. Children to fill his hall with laughter. To raise children and crops, that was a pleasant future. He'd seen enough of death and spilled enough blood.

By nightfall, Rorik had revised his opinion.

Wolf's Keep he expected to find in poor condition. What he failed to anticipate was Elissa—whom he recalled as little more than a babe herself—heavy with child, ravished and abandoned by Devere and stripped of her dowry and her pride both. She wept while she delivered news of Alain Devere's impending marriage to a neighboring heiress.

Simon was struck silent with fury by the news, although Rorik noted the concern in his manner as he helped Elissa find a chair and stood by her. So. Was that how matters stood? he wondered. Simon had always had a soft spot for the girl. Rorik had no objection to relinquishing his claim on her in favor of Simon. But Devere, that was another matter.

The baron had robbed him of home, and now Rorik was denied his wedding night as well while Devere anticipated his? Could the man be allowed to go his way and forget Elissa, robbed of her innocence and her wealth, left to survive however she could? Not that either he or Simon would allow her to suffer. But Devere could not have known that when he cast her off.

No. This outrage could not go unchallenged. It would serve the man well if his bride were stolen in return, Rorik thought.

By moonrise thought had grown to plan, and plan to action.

RORIK SLIPPED THROUGH THE window and slowly searched the chamber for his quarry with the patient, thorough eye of an experienced hunter and the guarded care of a veteran soldier. He spotted her easily in the bed once he lifted the draperies.

Moonlight touched her face with silver, and revealed the curve of an ivory cheek against a soft fall of midnight hair. The lady lay on her side, curled up like a sleeping child, her head pillowed on her hands. Her night rail lay twisted about her, and exposed a length of leg to the cool caress of the moon.

Rorik's breath caught as he gazed at her. He'd expected a woman, not a child. The consort of his enemy.

He hadn't expected her to look like an innocent in the arms of Morpheus.

Rorik hardened his heart and firmed his resolve. He'd have what he came for. He'd wreak his vengeance on Alain by stealing the man's bride, a fitting retribution. He'd have what was coming to him.

And he had a wedding night coming. Alain had robbed him of his. He would return the favor. Here, now, so there could be no question that he'd claimed the woman before taking her away. He wanted a wife. If he was denied the one he'd been promised, he would have this one. Ailiss, her name was. It suited her, he thought.

He did acknowledge that the woman he'd come to steal might not be pleased with his plan. Simon was forever telling him that his fearsome reputation and hard ways would not win a lady's love, but if she had been willing to marry Alain Devere, she could hardly consider him a worse husband. She might even view him as an improvement.

Rorik stripped and then set about securing his prize, his movements swift and sure in the darkened chamber. A length of silk served to gag the wench. Another covered her eyes, and still another bound her wrists together. The other end Rorik tied to the bedpost and he smiled at the convenience. By now his quarry was awake, although barely a minute had passed since he first set foot inside the bedchamber.

She struggled and managed a few good kicks before he caught her feet and ruthlessly tied them wide apart. Her strength both surprised and pleased him. He drew his small ornamental knife, used mainly for eating, but which now served to slit her garment from top to bottom. She froze at the cold touch of metal. Then Rorik stripped away the cloth, his eyes devouring the naked flesh revealed to his gaze.

She was a vision of erotic beauty, naked and spread for his pleasure, and Rorik burned to claim her. He would take those perfect breasts, that small waist, the graceful curve of her hips. He would take the softly furred mound between her thighs that lay exposed and unprotected, his to plunder. He would spend his seed in her body. He felt hunger rising, like none he'd ever known. A dark hunger, a need to dominate and demand submission.

Beneath the animal haze of his hunger, Rorik realized she was afraid. He could feel her fear like a living thing in the night as he lowered himself over her, trapping her with his weight. He could feel it as surely as he felt her soft breasts against his skin, and it didn't please him. Her breath came too fast, her heart pounded too fiercely and Rorik frowned, recognizing the signs of panic. He intended to seduce her into cooperating, not brutalize her.

She lay frozen beneath him until she felt the hard shaft of his cock against her thigh, seeking out and probing at the entrance to her body, and then her fear found expression in violent struggle. Rorik was hard-pressed to hold her down with his weight. As small as she was, she nearly succeeded in throwing him off.

Then he realized something else.

She wasn't fighting him. She had no fear of him. Her skin burned against his and the rich scent of her arousal filled the air. He knew if he tasted the pink flesh between her thighs, he would find her cream flowing for him. But she was fighting the silken bonds as if they were the living embodiment of every dark horror she knew or imagined. She fought so wildly that he feared she'd injure herself.

He wanted her bound. More than that, he wanted her submissive. But he couldn't allow her to hurt herself.

Rorik hesitated then removed the cloth that cut off her vision. Her wide eyes met his. Feral, golden eyes that sent a jolt of recognition through him. Dimly, he remembered seeing this before. Golden eyes in wild panic. Blood running from trapped appendages. Black hair that blended into the night.

A she-wolf, caught in a trap, another night long ago. The wolf had torn at herself in a frenzy to be free. She would have injured herself if he hadn't stopped her. To spare her that, he'd risked coming forward to free her. He hadn't been able to explain the impulse that drove him, but he couldn't see the creature suffer for the desperate need to be free.

He'd taken pity on the wolf and gained a vicious wound for his trouble. When he recovered, he found he'd gained something more. A dark legacy that slept inside him and awoke when needed, lending strength and instinct and heightened senses that had helped Rorik survive countless battles.

Every full moon it rose to ascendancy. The moon would be full in one more night. Already the wolf within prowled and pushed, awake and wanting to break free.

The hunger for this woman belonged to the wolf, Rorik realized. Not his human self. Was it the near-full moon or the woman who had woken his wolf? Her scent drew him like no other. Instinct demanded that he claim her.

He had known other women, but none had ever made the beast within him rise and demand to mate. It burned in him like a fever, and Rorik realized the touch of her skin against his had triggered this animal need to mate and to be acknowledged as the dominant one.

He stared down at her and she stared back at him, a trapped wild creature touched by moonlight. What was she?

Even as the question formed, he knew the answer. The woman and the wolf who'd torn his flesh that long-ago night were one.

TWO

As Rorik absorbed the truth, questions rose. How had she come to be here? Did Alain know what she was? Or had she kept her nature hidden from him while she bided her time and waited for the full moon to free her?

One thing he knew. She would tear open her wrists fighting for freedom and never feel the pain in her state, driven by an inner wildness that couldn't bear captivity. She would injure herself badly if he didn't stop her.

Rorik reached for the silken knot, but her struggles had tightened it beyond loosening. He drew the knife again and her struggles intensified. It took all his strength to hold her, but if he failed to keep her still, she'd cut herself on the blade instead of allowing him to cut the cloth. Rorik held her ruthlessly still and cut her hands free. Then he forced her arms apart and down, shackled by his hands.

She went still now that her hands were trapped only by his, but the rapid rise and fall of her breasts told him that his captive was far from calm. Would she submit to him now? Or scream for help if he removed the gag?

He could feel the hardened pebbles of her nipples against his chest. The scent of her heat intoxicated him. He wanted to bury his tongue in her quim and taste her juices. And then he wanted to drive his cock inside her hot, slick flesh and fuck her, spurting his seed into the depths of her body.

"Hush," Rorik murmured, holding her more easily now that she'd ceased her ferocious struggles. He held her gaze with his, willing her to be calm. "Hush, now."

It was like looking into the eyes of the she-wolf, Rorik thought in wonder. Animal wariness and animal cunning, combined with something primal and untamed, shone in her uncanny golden eyes. Looking into her eyes, resolve hardened in the depths of his soul.

This creature would never belong to Devere, or any other man. Never. She was his. He had come to claim her, and now she would know her mate.

A low growl escaped him and he felt her shiver as the sound danced over her skin. He lowered his head and let his teeth close on the soft skin at her throat. The wolf inside demanded that she acknowledge him as alpha. She made a low sound and went limp under him. Her head tipped back, exposing all of her vulnerable throat to him. His growl became one of triumph.

Her body shifted under his, hips arching up against him as if seeking contact with the broad head of his cock. Rorik released her throat and covered her torso with soft nips, kisses and licks, claiming her breasts, her nipples, moving lower to nuzzle the curve of her belly. He rose on his knees and looked down at her, naked and spread for him, the gleam of her juices visible on her quim in the moonlight.

He took her with his mouth first. He sought out the sensitive nub that hid in the slick folds of her flesh and sucked at it. She gasped and arched her back, offering herself more fully to him.

Rorik feasted on her quim, licking, sucking, devouring. He drove his tongue into her while she moaned and fisted her hands in his hair in a silent demand.

His little wolf wanted satisfaction. Rorik gave it to her, working first one finger, then two into her tight passage while he pleasured her with his mouth. The scent of her and the taste and feel of her slick flesh made his cock throb. She rocked her hips into him to meet the pressure of his invading fingers, opening for him, and then she came for him while he lapped up her cream. When he felt her inner muscles relax their grip on his fingers, he withdrew them.

Rorik rose above her and settled his cock between her thighs. The broad head of his shaft pushed against the slick flesh of her quim, softened and made ready for his entry. He pressed forward and felt her sex opening for him, stretching to accommodate him.

Holding her eyes as firmly as he held her slight body, Rorik drove himself into her, rending the slight barrier he expected. He knew that first thrust may have hurt her, but she didn't flinch or make a sound. He could have removed the cloth from her mouth without any fear that she'd raise an alarm. She was as soundless as the night.

Rorik kept still, knowing her silence didn't mean his swift taking of her virginity didn't pain her. He gave her body time to adjust to his invasion, to soften and relax. She was fully aroused, her quim swollen and slick for him. Now he waited for her to indicate that she was ready for his next thrust. The tight clasp of her sex gripping his cock made him want to drive into her again and again. The wolf inside him told Rorik that she burned with the same fever to mate.

"I am sorry if I hurt you, little one," he said softly.

She didn't move, blink or in any way signify that she heard, or that his words had any meaning to her. Nevertheless, Rorik knew she heard. Then she moved underneath him, her hips shifting to take him deeper, a clear invitation for him to continue.

Control snapped. The need to mate made him swift and urgent as he took her, claiming her irrevocably. He tried to be gentle. He tried to have a care for her slight size and untried body, but need burned too fiercely. She was his and the beast inside him would not go slowly. With every deep thrust he felt a force growing between them, felt a strange power building.

Rorik claimed his mate with driving fury. When he felt the inner muscles of her quim gripping his cock as she found her pleasure again, he let go and filled her tight channel with his seed in a violent spending that made him shudder and left him feeling as if the little she-wolf had ripped his soul from his body and taken it for herself.

Not that she looked like she wanted it. She looked shocked and confused, as if she couldn't imagine why she'd woken to find a strange man in her bed, or why she'd let him fuck her.

AILISS LAY UNDER THE alpha who had come to her, trembling with the aftershocks of pleasure and the still-surging force of the mating bond. So the tales were true. When mates touched for the first time the wolves within recognized each other and the two must join their flesh and become one.

Not as in a human marriage. Something older and deeper, a bond that once formed could never be broken. It was said the bonds were formed in another life and time and must re-form when the wolves are reunited with their mates. That their mates were predestined, chosen for all time during a previous and forgotten birth.

They lost the memory of that past life but they kept the ability to recognize their mates. That was the legacy of the human wolves.

Some of her kin never found their mates. They might be born separated by great distances. Ailiss had thought never to be reunited with her mate. She had been declared the property of a human male and given to him, the marriage to be formalized on the morrow. Her family had been unable to prevent the wedding without revealing their secret. How had her mate come to find her now?

She had felt him, sensed him, before she opened her eyes and saw him. And then he had blindfolded, gagged and bound her.

Underneath the euphoria of mating lay fury that he had overpowered her. But then, he was alpha. Instinct would demand he dominate, that she must submit to him. Her own instinct had demanded she submit, her body's recognition of him a separate thing from her mind or will.

Even now, with her feet still tied apart and her mouth gagged, her body burned for his to claim her again. She wanted his cock inside her, driving into her with deep, long strokes. She wanted him to possess her body and satisfy the animal hunger that had risen to meet his.

She, the one who so dearly guarded her freedom, who fought against any restraint, had lay back with her legs open with his bonds around her and spilled her juices while he lapped them up. And then, when he spilled himself inside her, she had creamed for him a second time, still bound.

Ailiss felt her slick juices flowing from her quim at the very thought.

A part of her delighted in this submission to her mate, her alpha. He hadn't harmed her, had freed her wrists when he understood her panic. Then he had overridden panic with pleasure, awakening the wolf within her, triggering the mating fever that swept over her.

It rode her still. She moved restlessly against the bonds. They prevented her from locking her legs around his waist, or from rolling to rise on her knees and offer her rear to him. His cock was still planted deep inside her quim and it wasn't enough. He hadn't taken enough of her.

Her mate withdrew from her and she wanted to shriek her fury at the loss. Her sex ached to be filled with his cock again and again. He finished untying her. He freed her legs, then her mouth and gathered her into his arms to hold her close to his heart.

"Little wolf," he whispered against her hair, "now it is done. You belong to me. And I keep what is mine." Triumph filled his voice. His hand followed the invitation of her parted thighs and cupped her quim, stroking the folds of her sex, dipping his fingers in the cream that flowed for him.

"So wet," he growled.

He thrust his fingers into her and Ailiss made a low sound of pleasure. Yes. That was better. She needed him to penetrate her. She moved her hips against his hand, arching her back, rocking into him, riding his fingers as they plunged into her quim.

Ailiss loved the fullness of his fingers thrusting into her, her sex opening and stretching for him. He rubbed at the tight bud of her clit with his thumb and she wanted to shriek her pleasure. And she wanted more.

She heard his soft laugh at her response. His thumb ground against her sensitive nub again and again while he worked her quim with his fingers. Ailiss felt her inner muscles begin to quiver, then clamp down on the fingers thrust deep inside her while she came again.

Rorik cradled his mate in his arms, his fingers still buried in her core. *Mine*. The wolf within all but howled its satisfaction.

Whatever the cost, he was taking his captive bride home, and he would fight the devil himself to keep her. She belonged to him. The fierce knowledge made him nearly euphoric in his possession. He would take her even if it meant war, and since she'd been promised to Devere, it undoubtedly would, Rorik wryly acknowledged to himself.

It was a good thing Wolf's Keep had sturdy defenses and ready, able men, well-trained and experienced in war. His men might even enjoy a bit of a siege to keep their spirits up and their hands in. Certainly they'd protested his decision to slip into Devere's holding on the eve of his wedding alone. They were spoiling for a fight and had no wish to be left out. He'd surely gain them one for this night's work.

She stirred against him and Rorik lay still as she touched him, first tentatively, then openly exploring him with curious hands. She touched the scars on his chest, then looked up at him and spoke for the first time. "You are Rorik, the knight they call the Fell Wolf, are you not? It was you I wounded. I never meant to hurt you, or force the change upon you. I was afraid and I struck out."

Her voice was pitched low with a husky timbre to it that pleased Rorik. The sound of her voice, the silk of her bare skin against his, the slick heat of her sex when it clasped his cock all pleased him.

He covered her hands with one of his. "I know. You were young. So was I, or I would have been more cautious."

"You are not angry?"

"Should I be angry that you gave me the strength and cunning to survive tournaments and wars?" Rorik asked her. "Or the instinct to recognize my mate?"

"You might not have been grateful. And you bound me." Her voice sounded both angry and hurt over his method of capturing her.

"I thought you might try to escape before I could persuade you to surrender your body to me. I had no wish to spend the night hours chasing you about the chamber and dragging you out from beneath the bed when we could use our time in more enjoyable ways."

"Then you knew what I was when you came?" she asked. She rose up on one elbow to see his face in the moonlight.

"No." He moved his fingers inside her and watched her reaction reflected in her eyes. They darkened and her lips parted slightly. "I knew that you were promised to Devere and he had taken the woman promised to me. It seemed fair that I take you in exchange."

"So you came here to hurt me. Or to get even with him." Her eyes shuttered and her face went still, all expression slipping away.

Rorik thrust a third finger into her with a low growl, asserting his possession of her. "I came for my due. You are mine, and if you prefer your promised husband to me you do not know him well. He would kill you. Elissa he could use and discard, she is too gentle to be any challenge to him, and her family has no power to threaten a baron. But he is not a stupid man. He would know that you posed a danger and he would have arranged an accident if he didn't simply murder you outright."

"He does not suspect my nature." Her eyes flew open again and Rorik saw rebellion in them.

"He does not believe in demon wolves, but I assure you he would know if you defied him, and that you had the will to cut his throat while he slept if he displeased you. He would never be able to control you. He would do his best to break you and failing that, he would decide you could not be allowed to live."

"You would not be afraid to sleep beside me at night?"

She was challenging him. Rorik laughed softly.

"I will tame you, Ailiss. And I will give you no reason to cut short my days on this earth." He moved his head to capture her lower lip with his teeth. He nipped at the sensitive flesh then released it. "I will give you so much pleasure you will not wish to deprive yourself of the source."

"I have no wish to die," she answered, sounding disgruntled.

"What do you mean? Do you believe I would harm you?"

She stared at him. "I mean that to cause your death would mean my own. We are mated. My life force is now bound to yours. I cannot be separated from you without growing weak, even dying if we are kept apart. I am stuck with you, caught forever in this trap, and you wanted me only because I was your enemy's prize."

Her face was expressionless, but her voice was bitter.

"Ailiss." Rorik slid his hand free of her and wrapped his arms around her, drawing her close. Instinct told him that the touch of his flesh against hers, as much of it as possible, would give her comfort.

A sound in the hall roused him to action. His mate was in danger if they lingered here.

Moving swiftly, Rorik rose and grabbed a garment from the chest in the chamber and dressed his silent prize in it, then wrapped her in his voluminous black cloak for warmth, frowning as he did so at the sudden loss of heat in her pale flesh.

She was too cold, as if the heat of their mating had burned out and left her chilled and shocked. He supposed she hadn't expected to be bound and gagged then ravished and abducted by an inhuman stranger on the eve of her wedding.

All things considered, he thought she was taking it rather well. Still, it alarmed him. He wrapped her as warmly as he could before taking up the rope he'd used to scale her wall, and climbed out the window, holding her cradled against his broad chest.

"Steady," he said softly, seeing fear flare in her eyes again. "Be still. I'll not drop you." At his words, her golden gaze dipped to the ground below, barely visible in the moonlight, and her already pale face blanched at the height.

"Hold tight to me," Rorik commanded. His mate obeyed, closing her eyes and burying her face in his shoulder without speaking.

It pleased him. She was wild, his little wolf, but she felt the bond between them and she knew him as surely as he knew her. Rorik pressed a light kiss on her forehead in reward. Then he lowered them slowly and carefully to the ground, playing out the rope and taking them over the distance in a series of measured drops.

The moonlit night was further evidence of Alain Devere's incompetence. Rorik never should have been able to breach the wall this night, never should have come close to stealing this treasure in his arms.

"Alain failed to guard you well," Rorik growled against her hair. "You may be certain I will not prove so careless. No man or wolf will take you from me."

She didn't answer. Rorik didn't expect her to. He left the rope as an announcement, in case the bloodstained sheets didn't serve well enough to notify all within the castle that the lord's bride had been claimed by another.

Melting into the night, he carried her to the place where Simon waited with the horses.

"You have her, then." Simon eyed Ailiss. "She looks pale. Have you been terrifying her with tales about her new home?"

"She doesn't frighten easily."

"Good choice for you to marry, then. I thought Elissa would expire from relief when the dread Fell Wolf released her from her duty."

"Elissa ought to fear that you'll talk her to death," Rorik growled then mounted his horse in one easy movement, not at all burdened by Ailiss's added weight.

The steeds moved off at their riders' silent urgings, making their careful way through the woods. Rorik had chosen the beasts for sure-footedness and endurance, as well as speed.

They would need all three this night.

THREE

THEY RODE AT A steady pace until the enemy holding lay several miles behind them. Then Rorik signaled Simon to ride ahead. He urged his own stallion to speed and adjusted the spoils of his victory in his arms, holding her securely. His arms braced her on both sides and the hard wall of his chest made a solid resting place for his prize. He wouldn't let her fall.

He concentrated on their flight and tried not to think of the unsatisfied ache in his loins, stirred by her nearness. He wanted her again. He wanted to take her in fierce sexual domination again and again, until he knew she carried his child.

Ailiss belonged to him now. He would keep her and defend her against all comers. She would bear his children. She was his mate. Animal need rose, reminding him that the same hunger burned in her. The need for touch, for closeness. Rorik knew she needed more contact with him to grow warm again.

She had pulled away from him when she realized why he'd come to her, and there had been no time to make her understand that human plans were irrelevant. Their wolves had chosen. She belonged to him. That meant everything. Devere meant nothing, other than the obstacle he presented to their legal marriage. An obstacle that would be dealt with swiftly and surely.

Rorik stroked and caressed her beneath the cape as they rode. She trembled and shuddered with need at his touch and Rorik laughed softly, teasing her breasts as they swelled in his hands, rubbing the tight buds of her nipples with his palms.

"You belong to me," he informed her boldly. He lifted her to allow one hand to raise her gown, part her thighs and cup the slick, soft flesh of her quim. "See how your cream flows for me?"

Ailiss refused to look, mute with rebellion, and Rorik laughed again. She was stubborn but she pleased him, and he knew very well he pleased her.

She pretended to ignore him while he fondled her breasts and hiked her skirt up higher to more freely admire her bared sex, swollen and pink from serving his cock, glistening with the cream his fingers coaxed from her.

He could feel heat returning to her skin as he touched her, but to warm her from the core she needed more. They had time enough, Rorik decided. He stopped the horse and lifted Ailiss to the ground.

She started to run, a clear challenge of his abilities. He caught her easily, dropping her to the ground with her skirt nearly over her head. The beast within wanted to draw it out, not let it end so soon. To chase and capture her, proving his worth as her mate.

On another night they would play that game. But not tonight. Tonight he wanted to keep her close, not to lose contact with her, as if on some instinctive level he feared the loss of his touch might injure her.

A swift hand freed his throbbing shaft and then he buried his cock in her again without preamble. She was ready for him, her sex opening to welcome his invasion.

"You see, my lady? You cannot escape me. I have claimed you." Rorik smiled at his prize and her golden eyes burned in anger. He wasn't daunted. She was his, and he'd win her surrender.

The need to physically possess her and make her his rode him and he drove his cock into her quim endlessly. She shared his need, whether she wished to or not, and he felt certain the cold shock she suffered meant she needed this. She needed the touch of his skin against hers, the heat of him inside her.

Her velvety flesh enclosed and sheathed his hardness, and Rorik closed his eyes at the almost unbearable pleasure taking her gave him. His hands closed over her breasts then tore aside the fabric that covered them to bare them to his loving assault.

Lips and hands paid homage to her soft breasts as he sank his cock into her quim again and again. He closed his eyes and roared as he spilled his seed deep inside her, while she moaned and writhed under him, the inner muscles of her sex milking his cock as she came with him.

Spent, he opened his eyes and met hers again in steady regard. "You are mine," he stated evenly. "Mine."

Ailiss glared back at him.

Rorik merely laughed and hugged her as if she'd uttered the sweetest of lover's endearments. He kissed her, grinding her lips against her teeth in a show of domination.

He'd never felt anything like this before, this need to totally possess a woman and overpower her. He wanted her sweet surrender. But never her defeat. He would never make Ailiss the loser in any contest. She was his mate, and her strength of will was a match for his. The wolf inside him understood that and it pleased both animal and man.

She was hot to the touch now, as if her body's vital reserves had been replenished by mating once more. Relief swept through him. "Your chill is gone," he said. "Do you feel strong enough to ride on?"

"Is that why you stopped?" She sounded surprised.

"You were so chilled when I dressed you. You said separation could weaken you, and I think so soon even the barrier of clothing made too much separation." Rorik frowned at her in the moonlight. "Are you stronger now?"

"Yes." Ailiss gave him a guarded look. "You risked this delay because you feared for me?"

"I did." He moved inside her, a gentle thrust, emphasizing their connection. "We stopped too soon earlier, I think. Mating is not meant to be interrupted."

"No," she agreed. "But we had no choice. I heard the sounds as well. We would have been discovered if we had lingered there."

"We cannot linger here, either." He raised a hand to her face and stroked it, cupping the curve of her cheek. "I regret the need for haste, Ailiss. I will make it up to you. I will show you how I cherish your body. How I cherish you. You are my mate, and you will be my wife."

"Your stolen wife." But she didn't sound angry now.

"You would rather I tried to win you with courtly protestations of love? By reciting poems to your beauty, or standing beneath your window to sing to you? You would despise a man who did those things." Rorik withdrew from her and stood, straightening his clothing as he spoke. "I am a man of war. Of action. I am more suited to a weapon than a lute. And I suit you, little wolf."

He offered her his hand and drew her to her feet then

straightened her dress. He wrapped his cloak tightly around her once more to keep her from taking another chill. "We can delay no longer," he said urgently. "Devere will follow. Come."

It was obvious in spite of her complaints that his mate preferred him to Devere. In her haste to avoid pursuit, Ailiss tried to mount his stallion by herself and Rorik winced, envisioning her delicate body suffering a savage kick from the trained warhorse. To his amazement, however, Goliath stood fast and endured her.

Perhaps Goliath knew she was like him from her scent. Animals had responded to him differently since his change. It stood to reason they would react to Ailiss in the same way.

Relieved that she was unharmed, Rorik seated her on the horse's back before he mounted behind her and set Goliath once more on a course to safety. He settled her between the cradle of his thighs and held her close. "Sleep now," he commanded. "I will keep you safe."

She curled her body into his. Her breathing deepened. After a while, he knew she slept.

That action was most telling. She would not sleep in his arms if she didn't trust him, no matter how tired she was. He smiled down at his sleeping mate, pleased beyond words. She was his, well and truly.

Rorik pressed a tender kiss on her forehead and she sighed softly. "Rest well, little one," he whispered.

She'd claimed him as surely as he'd claimed her, Rorik thought. She'd left her mark on him, so long ago. Perhaps the wolf within her had known then what was meant to be. He stroked the length of her midnight hair, wanting to offer her comfort as she slept. She saw mating as a trap with no escape now, but he could not believe she wouldn't come to see it in a different light as time went on.

Tomorrow night the full moon would rise. They would shed their human skins and then perhaps the wolves could sort matters out.

The thought of the two of them together in animal form made Rorik impatient for the passage of time to free them. He had been a lone wolf all these years. What would it be like to run and hunt beside his mate? He was eager to experience it, to share the wild freedom of the night with Ailiss.

AILISS SPENT THE DAY that was to have been her wedding day sulking about Wolf's Keep. Rorik had made it clear that she was to be his lady, accorded all respect the position entailed, and then gone off to consult with his men on matters of defense. He expected Devere to attack. Ailiss did not.

Open assault was not the baron's way. He had been granted her hand in marriage by a combination of bribery, threats and trickery. An open declaration of war, coming to meet his enemy in force, those were honest actions. While Rorik prepared for siege, she tried to guess what method of trickery he would use.

The puzzle also served to keep her mind occupied far from the touchy topic of her current status. The fact that the marriage she had never wanted had been prevented brought her only relief. But now she had a more permanent arrangement to deal with. A mate. A mate who had not looked for or wanted her.

The human side of her wanted to curl up and weep. The animal side was fast losing patience with her. Wolves were practical creatures. Hers saw that her mate was strong, fierce, able to defend her and any young they had. Further, a human marriage posed a grave risk. She could have been discovered. Rorik had saved her from that possibility. For that alone, she ought to be grateful to him.

He had also taken care to rouse her heat fully before mating with her, making the experience pleasurable. He had untied her when he understood her reaction to restraint. He had stopped midflight to take her again, giving her his strength, his heat, his essence when he knew she needed it.

She had been united with her mate, saved from a disastrous marriage to a human, and treated well. So why wasn't she happy?

Pride, Ailiss realized. It was a blow to her pride when she understood that Rorik hadn't sought her out, that in his eyes any woman would have done. He wanted a wife, he was taking one, and it simply happened to be her.

Her wolf side found this ridiculous. Had he known there were others like him? Had he ever believed he could find a mate, that such a thing existed? He knew nothing of their kind, and that was her own fault. She had wounded him and fled in fear, telling no one what she had done, leaving him to either die or adapt to the change and make his own way.

In fact, discovering who and what she was had to have come as a shock to him. He had expected a human woman. He seemed more than pleased to have found her instead.

Ailiss wandered the grounds while she thought. Rorik had made it clear she was free to do as she pleased and roam where she willed within the limits of safety he'd defined. She wasn't fool enough to rebel against caution. She stayed within the boundaries he'd dictated, but because she was distracted and divided internally, she failed to heed her inner wolf's warning until it was too late.

The snap of a twig underfoot made her look up, and then a blanket fell around her, blocking her sight and offending her nose with the musty scent that clung to the material. While she was trapped in the rough folds of fabric, she was grabbed up and carried. Ailiss fought her unseen assailant, caught him off balance as she threw her weight off to one side and nearly managed to escape. Then her abductor clouted her on the temple and she felt her body go limp as the world went dark.

FOUR

WHEN AILISS CAME TO herself, she was still in darkness. Then she realized night had fallen. Hours must have passed since she was taken. Where was she? She lay on the musty blanket that had been used to capture her. She recognized it by both its scent and the scratchy feel of the fabric. Without moving, not wanting to give away any sign that she was awake in case her captor watched, Ailiss extended her senses to learn all she could from sight, sound and scent.

She identified the Fell Woods easily and felt relief. She hadn't been taken far. That was good. If she'd been taken too far from Rorik, that alone might have assured her death already. He would be near. A fear she hadn't even known she possessed eased and Ailiss relaxed slightly. Her mate would not allow her to be taken from him. He would come for her. Perhaps he was already in pursuit.

He wasn't near enough to sense, however. She heard owls, other night creatures, the rustling of leaves and twigs, but caught only the scent of one male she knew, in addition to the scent of her unseen abductor. Alain Devere. The baron was close. He hadn't been the one to capture her, but she could reason out perfectly well what had happened. He had paid some man to find her alone, take her and bring her to him. Undoubtedly Devere planned to ambush Rorik when he came for her.

She was meant to serve as the bait in the baron's trap, while he waited with his accomplice. Devere wouldn't risk a fair fight with a knight of Rorik's experience.

That triggered another thought. Was she trapped? Ailiss moved her hands and feet imperceptibly, testing. She found ropes at her wrists and ankles. That was a difficulty. She fought down panic and forced herself to take slow, even breaths. Then she felt the moon rising and wanted to smile. There would be no difficulty at all in a few minutes more. Her paws were smaller than human hands and feet.

Her dress, however, would be a hindrance. Getting free of the folds of fabric she wore posed a greater complication than the ropes. Fortunately, her captor was available to serve as lady's maid.

She let out a low moan as if in pain and stirred, drawing the baron's attention.

"So. You're awake." He came to stand over her, leaving his accomplice to watch for Rorik. "Such a tragic tale this will make. Poor Ailiss, kidnapped on the eve of your wedding then killed by your lover before I could free you. I admit I had intended to arrange your tragic end after our marriage, but this opportunity is too good to pass up. I wonder, should I kill your lover first, or make him watch while I rape you?"

"No! Don't touch me!" Ailiss whimpered.

Devere gave her a cruel smile and drew his ornamental dagger. "Let us see what lies beneath that gown."

So predictable, Ailiss thought. She had taken care never to be alone with the man, but his nature had been clear to her. If their wedding had taken place, it would have been a race to see which of them could kill the other first. Since he had never seen her as anything but a meek, biddable female, Ailiss felt confident that she had the advantage. She would have trembled to play her part better but feared the knife would slip if she did, so she settled for making weeping noises while keeping still.

The gown fell away, leaving her naked.

The light of the full moon touched her skin and Ailiss felt the transformation begin.

A sudden noise from behind him made the baron turn his head in the direction of the sound. When he turned back, he saw only the rope, still knotted, lying on the otherwise empty blanket with the ruined and abandoned gown.

Ailiss blended into the woods and waited for Rorik to come into view. He was close, almost close enough to see. And then he was there, a great wolf running full-out in the darkness. She moved, just enough for him to see her. She didn't have to tell him there were two men ahead, he could hear and smell them as well as she could.

One for each of us, she thought, and dropped her jaw in a canine grin.

The men were armed with bows as well as swords. It wouldn't be too easy. But they wouldn't expect to find themselves fighting wolves instead of a man, wolves who knew weapons and could think.

She heard a shout and knew they'd been spotted. The man who had captured her nocked an arrow into his bow. He was looking toward Rorik and she realized he hadn't seen her, hidden in the deeper shadows. She ran forward, choosing her angle for attack. He saw her when she burst into view a split second before he could loose his arrow. Ailiss leapt for his throat and made certain it was the last thing he would ever see.

She wheeled and looked for Rorik, saw him circling Devere, who had his sword out. Toying with the man. Drawing out his fun. She let out a soft *humph* and crouched to watch, ready to leap to her mate's defense if he needed her.

Rorik danced about Devere, worrying him, staying easily out of reach of the sword, leaping in to wound and draw blood and then back out of striking range. At first Ailiss thought he was simply bleeding the man to toy with him, then she saw the pattern. Devere was being disabled, one major muscle group at a time, as Rorik chose his targets. He left the hamstrings and Ailiss knew when the man could no longer hold or swing a weapon, Rorik intended him to run.

Ah. A chase. She approved. It came all too soon, the sword falling from Devere's now-useless hand, and then Rorik snapped at his legs. The man turned and fled. Rorik let him get a head start and Ailiss waited for him to begin the hunt before falling in behind him. They ran in silence, following not just the scent but the crashing sounds of Devere's panicked flight.

Rorik let him run until his steps slowed nearly to stumbling. Then he leapt, brought the man down and stood over his chest.

"It cannot be," Devere gasped out. "Stories. Legends."

Ailiss came forward and stood beside her mate, letting the man see her eyes and fur and make of it what he would. His eyes widened in disbelieving comprehension.

Then Rorik finished him off.

He turned to her and Ailiss knew what he wanted next. Another hunt, this one not lethal. There were matters to be resolved between them still, and a contest of skill, cunning and endurance was a step in that direction.

Ailiss sprang into the woods, beginning a game of chase with the sure knowledge that Rorik would catch her. But she intended to make him work for it.

FIVE

THEY SLIPPED BACK INTO Wolf's Keep near dawn and Rorik led the way to his chamber. It felt strange to become human again, the shift in balance seeming unnatural at first. Ailiss entered the room with slow steps, adjusting. Rorik closed the door and stood beside her, watching her.

They had run for hours in the woods. He had caught her in the end, but it hadn't been easy and she had very nearly succeeded in evading him until the moon set. Their game had left them both exhilarated rather than exhausted, and it could have only one conclusion.

"Did he hurt you?" Rorik asked.

Ailiss blinked, the question so unexpected it took her a moment to understand his meaning. "No. The man who kidnapped me gave me a good headache, but the worst thing they did was force me to endure having my head wrapped in a smelly blanket."

Rorik's mouth twitched in humor. With a heightened sense of smell, a foul odor was indeed difficult to endure, but hardly injurious.

"Then are you up to another challenge?" he asked.

"What did you have in mind?" Ailiss asked, feeling her pulse quicken and her quim swell and grow slick with anticipation. She knew very well what sort of challenge he wanted.

Instead of answering, he sprang toward her. Ailiss dodged to the side, evading him. He feinted one direction and Ailiss attacked instead of defending, going low, her shoulder aimed into the side of his thigh while her arms locked behind his knees. She nearly succeeded in bringing him down, but he recovered his balance and reached down to pinch her nipple.

She squealed in surprise and let go of him in a reflexive move to protect herself. He laughed and bent down, scooped her up and tossed her onto the bed. She slid off the other side and faced him with the bed between them, grinning.

Ailiss knew how their play would end, but this was a side of Rorik she hadn't expected. If he had a desire to play rough in the bedchamber, she could only assume he'd never had the opportunity to indulge it before. He'd have to be too careful of a human partner. It was too easy for the wolf's strength to turn pleasure into pain. With her, he wouldn't have to check himself.

Rorik feinted one direction. She moved opposite to counter, and he leapt over the bed, his arms closing around her. Ailiss laughed as he swung her around and threw her onto the bed again, this time following her down and trapping her beneath his weight.

She twisted and broke free, rolled over him and leapt away. He dove for her and brought her down to the floor with a crash. She went still as if surrendering and tapped him to indicate she wanted him to move off her.

"Did you think I would fall for that?" he asked her. He nuzzled her neck and then raked her with his teeth. She shuddered underneath him as heat flooded her body. His weight pinned her to the floor, the scent of him covered her, and she felt his hard cock against her bare buttocks.

"No, but I thought it worth trying." Ailiss arched up against him in silent invitation.

"Ah, so now you want me, after leading me on a chase all night long." Rorik levered himself up into a sitting position and scooped her into his lap, still facedown. "Time to teach you a lesson."

He delivered a stinging slap to her bare buttocks and Ailiss jolted in surprise. It brought a rush of blood to her quim and made her muscles clench. She squirmed to press her sex against him. Rorik secured her across his thighs so that she couldn't gain pressure where she wanted it and Ailiss made a low sound of frustration. He laughed and spanked her again. She wiggled and fought to get loose while he slid a hand beneath her and stroked the sensitive nub between her thighs.

The combination of his hand stimulating her quim from below while his other hand slapped her bare buttocks from above had her squirming and then bucking in his lap as she sought to gain her release. Just as she felt the waves of pleasure begin, he stopped. Ailiss let out a small scream and twisted in his arms.

She bit and clawed at him hard enough to draw blood as he wrestled her down onto her back and settled his cock between her thighs. He made no move to enter her, and she writhed under him in frustration.

"You made me wait for it for hours," he growled. "Your turn to wait now."

Ailiss locked her legs around his waist, lifted her hips and forced the head of him into her slick folds.

He pinched her nipple in retaliation and she gasped as the added stimulation, on the fine border between pleasure and pain, sent another rush of heat through her. "Rorik. Now."

He drove into her with one hard, fast thrust. She was already climaxing as he entered her. He pinched her nipple hard once more and she felt the waves of pleasure rippling through her again and again as he took her with furious force. When he spilled himself inside her, he threw his head back and roared his release.

Afterward they lay spent and gasping for breath, still entwined.

It had been a night of revelations. Her mate had fought for her, fought beside her and then fought with her in a sensual contest that proved he considered her his equal. He had not checked himself in their chase. It had taken all her speed and skill to evade him. And in wrestling with her, he hadn't given her any advantage. He had paid her the ultimate compliment, trusting her to be his match as well as his mate.

Rorik had shown her what she needed to see, that no other woman would ever do for him. Only with her could he fully be himself. Both selves, as she could fully be herself with him, in both of her forms.

She was well and truly caught in his sensual trap and never wanted to be free of him. Ailiss nuzzled his throat and slipped into sleep, sure of him and of their future.

One month later . . .

RORIK FOUND HIS MATE taking her ease in the deep shade of the woods. She leaned against a tree, her knees drawn up to her chest, bare feet visible from beneath the hem of her gown.

He spotted her shoes in a nearby heap and smiled. Shoes were a source of incessant complaints from his mate. They pinched. They annoyed. They kept her from feeling the ground beneath her feet. She went barefoot at every opportunity.

Ailiss looked up when she heard him coming toward her.

"There are wolves in these woods," Rorik informed her, still smiling.

"Really?" Her eyes widened.

"Truly. Dangerous wolves. If one spotted you, he might want to eat you up."

Ailiss put a hand to her chest in mock fright. "Ohhh. Not that. What should I do?"

"You could try to run, but it might make the wolf hungrier." Rorik looked down at her. "I suggest you surrender to the inevitable. Lift your skirt and spread your legs."

She let her knees fall open but didn't raise her skirt. "First tell me what you have there."

"This?" He gestured at the very visible bulge of his erection. "I think it speaks for itself."

"No, in your hand." She waved in the direction of it.

"Ah. This." Rorik offered it to her, then sprawled beside her on the ground and slid his hand beneath her skirt. "This documents all the details of our marriage. Your family seems quite pleased with the arrangement."

"Hmm." She handed it back to him and gave him a measuring look. "You are a brave knight. You know, the last man who was to have married me died. Quite mysteriously. Here in these very woods."

"No mystery there at all," Rorik grunted. "A wolf tore the man's throat out. Exactly what the fool deserved for wandering about in the woods at night."

"He tried to steal me from you." Ailiss sounded indignant all over again, and Rorik wondered if she wished he'd killed Devere more slowly.

"To be fair, I stole you from him first." Rorik stroked his hand along the soft skin of her inner thigh and then lightly traced the folds of her sex, bare to him beneath the cover of her skirt.

"I wanted to be stolen by you." Ailiss raised her skirt so they could both watch. Her quim was already growing swollen and slick for him. He thrust a finger into her and she sighed in pleasure. "You captured me twice. You deserved to keep me."

"I let you go the first time." Rorik thrust a second finger into her, preparing her for his cock. "I will never let you go again."

"What will you do with me?" She smiled at him, her lips curved in humor, her cheeks flushed with desire, and Rorik felt his heart turn over. He would never tire of the sight of her, the sound of her voice, the scent of her skin. In her human form or the shape of a wolf, she enchanted him. She matched his strength, his will, his pride. And his love.

"Claim you."

He lowered his mouth to her and tasted the cream that flowed for him. He suckled the swollen nub that hid in the folds of her sex until she moaned. His fingers thrust in and out of her quim while he licked and sucked at her. The rich scent of her arousal made his cock throb in anticipation. When he felt her nearing orgasm, he stopped and withdrew his fingers.

She made a low sound of protest.

Rorik nudged her hip. "On your belly."

Ailiss rolled over, her movements slow and sinuous. She tugged the fabric of her skirt down to protect her skin from the ground, but raised it up in back, baring her rear to him. He knelt behind her and moved her legs apart, then raised her up onto her knees so that he could see the pink, swollen folds of her quim, exposed and vulnerable.

Rorik traced the graceful line of her spine with his hands then cupped the curves of her naked bottom. The full shape of it tempted him and he gave it an experimental squeeze. He felt her respond and knew he could explore more of this territory. He toyed with her buttocks and traced a finger between the round globes, down to the tight rosy opening he could just reach with her thighs slightly apart. He stroked it lightly and felt her shiver in response.

So. That pleased her. Rorik slid his hand lower, cupped her naked quim and coated his fingers with her natural lubrication. Then he slowly, gently worked the tip of one finger into her anus. She let out a soft sigh of pleasure mingled with surprise. He stroked in and out of the tight opening while she arched her back a little more to give him better access.

Rorik leaned over her so he could nip sharply with his teeth at the curve of her neck where it joined her shoulder. He reached down with one hand to free his cock then guided it to the slick opening of her sex.

"I am going to fuck you," he said, pleasuring her ass while he prepared to fill her quim with his cock and his come. "Right here, beneath this tree, in these woods. I'll take you on your hands and knees."

"Yes." She thrust her hips back, forcing the head of his cock to enter her. Rorik pressed forward, entering her inch by inch, until his shaft was buried inside her as far as it could go with his hand barring full entry. The hot, tight clasp of her body gave him such satisfaction, such a sense of completion.

"Mine," he growled. He felt her tight muscles gripping his cock, smelled her arousal, felt her surrendering to his joint possession of her quim and the tighter opening that gripped his finger. The position would make it awkward to continue the dual penetration so Rorik left his exploration of her tempting rear for another time and gripped her hips with his hands instead.

Then he took her hard and fast. When he began to spurt his seed deep into her body's core, she buried her face against her arm to muffle her cries of pleasure while she milked his cock.

Spent, Rorik lowered his torso over hers and rested his head on her back, his cock still buried deep inside her. It was risky to linger like this, he knew. They could be discovered. But he stayed there a moment longer, unwilling to withdraw from her.

"Do you still consider this a trap?" he asked her.

Ailiss seemed content with him. He knew she enjoyed their bed games and whenever he wanted to play rough she gave as good as she got. Her response was as wild and untamed as her wolf's nature and she was as quick to laugh with him as she was to attack him in play. Yet some part of him worried that she might still resist or resent their bond.

She arched her back and pushed her hips against his, grinding him deeper into her quim. "I consider this a miracle. Tonight the moon will be full again and we'll both be free."

"I'll chase you again," Rorik promised.

"I'll let you catch me," Ailiss teased.

He nipped at her neck and growled. "I'll always catch you."

She let out a soft sigh. "I depend upon it."

Rorik wrapped his arms around her and rolled with her onto their sides, slipping out of her in the process. "This is where it began, you know. You marked me here."

"I did." She sounded pleased with herself.

"I saw you when it happened." He stroked her hips and belly as he spoke.

"Of course you saw me. I was the little black wolf springing out of the trap and ripping your chest open," Ailiss said.

"That, too. But for a moment, I saw something else. A golden-eyed woman with black hair flowing down to her waist. It's why I didn't move back or strike you to defend myself. You leapt at me as a wolf but I saw the woman."

Ailiss wiggled out of his hold so she could roll to face him. "You did?"

"I did. Simon saw only the wolf, but I think from that night on I knew I'd find you again."

She raked her nails down the front of his shirt, hard enough to hurt. "Which is why you intended to honor your arranged marriage first, and then decided to steal a wife for revenge when that plan fell through."

"What would you say if I told you I believe the wolf within knew what I would find when I stole into that room to capture you?" Rorik asked her.

She laid her open hand over the flesh that she'd scarred years before, hidden beneath his shirt, and spoke slowly. "I would say I believe it."

"You knew, too. The animal side of you knew when you bit me."

"Yes." She looked up at him. "I didn't understand. Not with my human side. I thought you'd done me a kindness and in return I'd done a terrible thing. Most humans lack the ability to change. To them our bite is death, not new life. Then I heard the stories of a dark knight said to have the soul of a wolf and I knew you'd lived."

"I did." He smiled at her and tugged her closer so he could kiss her with lazy thoroughness. "I have no wish for any other life, or any other mate. You are mine, and that is as it should be. All is well."

"I am yours," Ailiss agreed. She kissed him back, and then neither of them said anything more for hours.

STOLEN GODDESS

Tawny Taylor

One

KYLIE MANNINGS HATED SATURDAY nights. They reminded her of things she'd just as soon forget, like the time she'd gotten so drunk she'd tripped over a crack in the sidewalk and broken her ankle. Or the time she'd gotten a speeding ticket from a good-looking cop who had no appreciation for the risks of being late for a night of club-hopping with the girls. Or Adam Hubbard, the tall, dark-haired hunk of manliness she'd recently made an ex-boyfriend.

Yeah, Saturday nights sucked.

The ankle had eventually healed. And after paying AAA an atrocious amount for approximately thirty-six months for car insurance, along with a tidy sum to the city, the ticket fiasco was finally over. But the final issue—that of said ex-boyfriend—was still fresh in a "life sucks" kind of way. The kicker—it shouldn't have happened.

In this day and age, Kylie figured, a girl shouldn't have to choose between wedded bliss and a career. It was only her luck that she'd dated a guy who would put her in precisely that position—where she'd have to choose. He'd done that, and in the end they'd both lost. Big time.

As much as she liked Adam, just up and moving to the other

side of the world wasn't possible now, not with her career finally taking the turn she'd hoped for. Years of planning were at stake. Planning and hard work, not to mention some serious ass-kissing.

This was not just any little promotion. This was a once-in-a-lifetime promotion. Starting Monday morning she was vice president! Vice president of Sales and Marketing for a fastener manufacturer who catered to, or more like indulged, the Big Three. Anyone who knew the automotive industry knew how unlikely it was for a woman to end up in a position more powerful than office manager. A more likely position was legs spread, flat on her back under the other three vice presidents of the company. Somehow, by some small miracle, she'd sidestepped the first and avoided the latter.

In all honesty, Kylie expected to see a flock of pigs flying south at any moment.

The fact that it was Halloween and she was home alone, sitting on her front porch and waiting for kids who didn't seem to be coming didn't help her glum mood at all. Six feet four, two hundred twenty pounds of sin wrapped in Tommy Hilfiger, Adam had always made a big deal out of every holiday. But Halloween was his all-time favorite. Last year, he'd made her dress up as Eve—of biblical fame. Together, sporting matching felt fig leaves, they'd handed out bucketloads of candy to trick-or-treaters, and later went party-hopping before returning home to enjoy hours of sex.

How things had changed in one year! She sure as hell wasn't going to get any sex this year.

She missed Adam, even though she knew she hadn't loved him. While their sex life had rocked, there'd been something missing in the emotion department. Not that she had reason to complain. Her lack of deeper feelings had made it easy to keep their relationship casual. Casual was good. Casual didn't interfere in plans, careers.

Not happy about the direction her thoughts were headed, she shook her head, like it would knock those unhappy thoughts away, glanced at her watch for the umpteenth time—in twenty minutes—and wrapped her jacket tighter around herself. The wind had picked up and gusts of arctic air were slapping her cheeks and tossing her hair. Her nose and fingers were growing numb, fast. So was her butt, thanks to the fact that her porch was the size of a postage stamp and wouldn't accommodate a chair. It was amazing how cold concrete got.

This was stupid. Lame. Pathetic. So what if she'd planned for this night for weeks? Shopped the candy sales. Picked up all the "good" candy so the kids would beam with joy. Why couldn't she just admit that sometimes plans didn't work out, and move on?

After checking up and down her street for signs of little fairies, devils or dragons, she reluctantly picked up the bowl of candy and headed inside. No reason to sit outside on the porch and freeze like a dork with no life. She had a life. She had a career. And she had things to do, besides sitting in the cold and risking frostbite on her ass. She left the porch light on in case any kids did wander her way, and threw herself on the couch with a book. Not quite a chapter into her reading, the doorbell rang for the first time.

Although she had determined ages ago that she was not mother material—hand in hand with kids came chaos, she'd seen it with her friends—she still adored handing out candy to cute kiddies in costumes on Halloween. Glad to finally have some visitors, she scooped up fistfuls of wrapped chocolate bars, donned a "Happy Halloween" smile and threw open the door to greet them.

The minute she opened the door she had a funny feeling. The kids standing on the other side weren't your typical trick-or-treaters. There were two of them, dressed head-to-toe in black. They towered over her by at least six inches. Probably out-weighed her by a hundred pounds each.

They sure were making kids big these days.

"What do your mothers feed you?" she asked, smiling despite a swelling sense of doom. "Whole cows?" Prepared to dole out the Snickers bars melting in her fists, she looked down at their hands. That was when she realized they were not trick-or-treating. Instead of pillowcases loaded with suckers and Twix, these guys were holding rope.

Out of sheer instinct, she threw the candy—not that a half-dozen Snickers would hurt a couple of giant thugs—jumped backward and swung the door, but it was too late, they were inside and on top of her before she could scream, "I have Mace."

Thanks to a significant size and strength disparity, and the fact that she had been lying and had no Mace, she lost the wrestling match pretty quickly. She also lost something else, thanks to a smelly rag smashed up against her mouth and nose.

She lost consciousness.

"YOU'LL HAVE TO BE punished," someone said. Someone male. Someone close. Someone with an extremely deep voice. She liked deep voices. And punishment didn't always have to be a bad thing.

Anxious to see who was promising discipline with the deep bass voice, despite the pounding in her head, Kylie dragged her eyelids up, uncovering eyes that felt like they'd been rolled in sand. Everything was still very hazy. Dark. Strange. She felt groggy, sick, like she'd overdosed on Nyquil. She tried to sit up but realized she couldn't. Her hands were tied up over her head. While wriggling her arms, she tested her feet. They too were tied.

What the fuck?

She could see there were only two people in the tiny room—her and the man who had spoken. He was completely nude. Nude and sporting a hard-on that suggested he was quite happy to see her, yet he glared at her, rage pulling his features into a tense mask. Oh boy. This was not good. Was he going to rape her?

A girl who'd lived in some rough neighborhoods growing up, she went into survival mode—decided pretty quickly she'd better go easy with this guy, try to gain his trust. She'd soothe his ruffled feathers. Pretend to go along with whatever he wanted until she found the opportunity to escape. He looked furious. And he looked strong. At the moment, she was not in the ideal position to defend herself. Yes, playing the waiting game was definitely in order.

However, her carefully laid plans changed when a quick glance down verified what she'd suspected almost immediately after waking—she was naked.

Embarrassment and shame swept through her body, churning in her belly with a good amount of anger. What right did this guy have? Taking her from her home, stripping her, holding her hostage! It was downright . . . medieval! No, it was cavemanish. She should be the one glowering. Despite her fear about the consequences, she gave the Neanderthal a glare right back.

"I can see your attitude hasn't improved yet," he said sharply.

"Huh? Yet? How would you know about my attitude? You've never seen it before." She had to get out of there. Now. She gritted her teeth and yanked at the rope holding her wrists.

"Of course I've seen this attitude before." Something flashed through his eyes. "How dare you lie to me!"

"Lie?" Was this guy nuts? Or was this some kind of sick game? "You couldn't have seen my attitude before because we've never met. I have no idea who you are or what I'm doing strapped to this fucking bed, naked. How dare *you*!"

Whatever he was going to say—and she knew he was about to speak because he'd opened his mouth—got caught somewhere between his chest and tongue. He snapped his jaw shut and, turning, threw open a door.

The two thugs who'd masqueraded as trick-or-treaters stepped inside. The three of them—the Thug Brothers and the Neanderthal—huddled together, whispering, pointing, nodding collective heads. Then they stalked toward her.

She had to say, she quickly gained a new appreciation for how turkeys felt on Thanksgiving Day.

Despite the fact that the bindings holding her wrists and ankles were tighter than bear traps, she fought them fiercely. As a result of her frenzied yanking and thrashing, the rope burned her skin, cutting deeply until she had to stop. She was worn out and a victim of agonizing pain, after only a few minutes of struggling and a couple shallow burns. Sad. She was a wimp! How would she ever get out of this alive? She vowed to get back to the gym if she lived through this ordeal.

Her bare breasts rose and fell with each racing gasp. Her wrists were killing her. Her heart was heavy with the knowledge that she was entirely at the men's mercies. Yet she refused to acknowledge defeat. Still breathless and totally embarrassed by her nudity, she scraped up what was left of her pride, lifted her chin and stared the tallest one—the Neanderthal—right in the eyes.

To hell with placating him! She felt as raw as her wrists. Her emotions were taking over, clouding her thoughts. Anger. Fear. Confusion.

That had never happened to her before. That confused her more.

"I am certain this is her. But she insists—"

"Of course it's her," Thug Brother One said, pointing at the tattoo she had on her hip bone. The design was one-of-a-kind, an intricate series of swirls and curlicues she'd dreamed about once a long time ago and had sketched a bazillion times after. In notebooks, on scrap paper, in her address book. "She has the mark."

"Mark? That's just a doodle," she said. "My doodle. No one else has ever seen it before." Just her luck, they thought it was some kind of brand or something.

"We checked before bringing her," Thug Brother Two said, nodding.

The asshole holding her hostage nodded and let the men out, then turned, his jaw set.

She'd seen many a man with that expression before. Men who were determined to sink a putt, or close a deal, no matter what. As much as she hated to admit it, it was an expression that had turned her on in the past, especially when she'd seen it on Adam's mug. A shameful thing, but here too it had an effect on her. The firm set of the Neanderthal's jaw had her squirming, even though she had no idea who he was or what he wanted with her.

It was time to be honest with herself, she decided, since she could very well be facing some life-altering events, if not life-ending. Despite her shock, anger and fear, she hadn't been able to ignore the Neanderthal's shocking good looks. This guy was straight out of her fantasies, right down to the dark curly hair that was a little too long to be fashionable. Physically, he was a combination of all her favorite movie stars. Vin Diesel's body. Antonio Banderas's coloring and hair. A touch of Orlando Bloom. She'd never in a million years dreamed of getting busy with a guy who looked as good as that, like he'd walked off a movie set. This guy made Andy—er, Adam!—look like dog meat.

"You say you don't remember me. So, I guess I have no other choice." He stood next to her, too close. His gaze smoothed up and down her body like a sensual caress.

"I didn't say I don't remember you. I said I've never met . . . you . . ." She felt herself melting. Her body's instantaneous reaction pissed her off and she was forced to explain it away in a rush of empty excuses to maintain her self-respect. Kylie Mannings was a strong woman. A woman with a backbone. A mind. She did not appreciate being treated like a brainless hunk of prime rib laid out on a hibachi. He stared at her breasts and her nipples tingled, sending little zaps of wanting down her spine. "Urgh!"

Yes, she had a mind. Even if her tongue was tied in knots at the moment and she was talking like a Neanderthal.

"I'll simply have to reacquaint us," he said, sounding—and looking—downright pleased. He licked his lips. She stared. He had nice lips. Full for a guy. They looked soft. Yummy. He leaned closer and ran a single fingertip down the center of her belly.

Even as she shuddered with desire, she growled, "Like hell you will. Don't you dare touch me or I'll scream. Loud."

His chuckle sent shivers through her body, good shivers, the kind she hadn't indulged in since Adam left. And the smile, well, that nearly put her in a coma. "I must say, I've never seen this side of you. You've always been such a . . . compliant wife."

Her tongue sprung free of its knot. "What? Wife? Did you say wife?" she interrupted. Why would he think she was his wife?

Was that what he was saying? No. She'd misunderstood. There could be no other explanation.

He frowned. She had to admit, the smile did a lot more for her than the frown. "Yes, of course I said wife," he said. "We've been married for almost six years." He leaned forward, closer, closer, closer, until his breath warmed her lips. He was going to kiss her? He thought she was his wife. Shouldn't she try to correct him before he did something crazy, like lay those lips on hers? Yes. Yes, she should. "Don't you remember me?" he asked. He blew a cool stream of air on her mouth and a rush of warmth blazed along her nerves. She closed her eyes and sucked in a gasp. "We've been very, very happily married," he added. His lips brushed gently across hers in a light, teasing kiss. "Until you left."

Her resolve crumbled. They'd figure out all that wife stuff later.

"Why'd you leave me?" he asked.

Good question.

"I know everything about you," he continued. "Like how you love me to pinch your nipples . . ." While she lay shamefully still, he closed a forefinger and thumb over each taut bud and squeezed until she was near tears and her heart was skipping beats and her pussy was wet and hot and ready. ". . . like this and then kiss them." He leaned over her and closed his warm mouth over one still-stinging nub, taking away the pain with slow, lazy swipes of his velvety tongue.

Oh, she wasn't lying so still any longer. But she wasn't exactly trying to get away, either.

His hand cupped her other breast, kneading its softness and teasing the nipple until she was begging for relief, until cream was making her pussy slick and she was writhing under him. Hot, tense, wanting.

This was insanity! She'd never had sex with a stranger. Not even when she was stupid-drunk in college and everyone around her was hopping in the sack with whomever they could get their hands on. She'd always been careful, thought things out before she'd slept with a new lover. Not even Adam had been able to get past her defenses the first night—though he did try! She'd made the poor man wait almost a full month before she'd given in. She could just imagine how many nights he'd walked into his house, nursing a set of aching testicles from the tormenting she'd given them.

But, oh, the agony she was facing now! Her pussy was burning up. Empty. Her body was aching for completion she instinctively knew only this man could give her. She trembled with need. This wasn't just her average need. This was need beyond words.

Would it be so wrong to have sex with this man?

She shook away the thought, rocked her head from side to side. Why was she even considering this now? It made no sense. He'd had her kidnapped! Sure, he was under the false impression that she was his wife. So really, in his eyes, he'd just paid a couple of thugs to get his wife back. Was that kidnapping? Perhaps he'd thought she was in trouble.

"I know how you love to play chasing games. Is that why you left? Was it another game?" His expression changed, from confusion to wicked pleasure. "That's what it was, wasn't it? You were waiting for me to find you. Discipline you." He traced a circle around one nipple with an index finger then drew little wavering lines on her lower belly. "You're so naughty. I want to fuck you."

Oh, God! Why was her pussy clenching around its own heated emptiness? Her hips rocking back and forth in time with the waves of wanting crashing through her body? This wasn't her husband.

Actually, she knew why, but she wasn't ready to accept it yet.

He left her side and walked around the foot of the bed to kneel on the mattress and wedge his knees between her legs. She dropped her head back and tightened her spine with anticipation. She couldn't look at him, couldn't watch as his gaze traveled her length, settled at the thick patch of curls between her thighs, slick with the evidence of her need. He set his hands on her knees then slowly slid them higher, up her thighs until they rested on either side of her hips and his thumbs were dipping into the sensitive creases on either side of her center. "Only I know what makes you wet. What makes you tremble with desire. What makes you beg for more."

That was it. Her brain raised the white flag, admitting defeat. Now she was ready to accept why she was considering sleeping with this man, this . . . stranger.

What he said was true, somehow he knew her. Oh, yes he did. At least he knew her body. He knew how to touch her, where to touch her. He knew how ticklish she was, how a kiss just above her pubic bone made her squirm. How a stroke to the sensitive skin at the backs of her knees would make her beg for more. What to say to make her tremble.

Could she be wrong about not knowing him? Had they met somewhere? Made love? How could that be?

When he dragged his tongue over her folds, she decided she didn't give a damn how it could be. She'd sort it all out later.

For once in her life, Kylie Mannings would act on a whim. She'd forget about plans and consequences. She'd follow her heart. Just this once. To hell with logic.

As if he sensed her acquiescence, he stopped the tender

loving care he was so generously lavishing on her pussy and untied her feet. She was beyond thrilled when he gently forced her knees to bend and pushed them back until her pussy was wide open for him. Oh, yes, it felt so good. So right. She moaned.

"That's it, love. Turn yourself over to me. Let yourself go."

She couldn't do anything but. There wasn't a nerve ending that wasn't tingling. There wasn't a muscle fiber that wasn't pulled tight. There wasn't a sensation that wasn't amplified to the extreme—smell, taste, touch. She was drowning in a blissful sea of sounds and touches and scents. She could hear the sharp intake of breath when she tipped her hips to silently plead for more. She could feel the cool, smooth texture of the sheets underneath her. And the spicy, all-male scent of him was making her dizzy. Like an addict, she kept dragging in deep breaths through her nose, wishing the smell would linger there, where she could enjoy it forever.

His tongue found her clit and danced over it in a series of swift flickers that had her bucking and pleading and panting. She was so hot, burning up from head to toe, like from a fever. It was too much, yet not enough. She wanted it to end, the torture. And she wanted it to go on forever.

"Fuck me," she begged. She wrapped her fingers around the rope and squeezed. The rough fibers scratched her palms but the slight pain only amplified the pleasure. "Please, oh please. Fuck me."

"Very well, wife." His voice was low, gritty, and she guessed he was as desperate for completion as she was.

She nearly wept with gratitude when a few stuttering heartbeats later she felt him kneel at her bottom, lift her hips and prod at her pussy with his cock. He didn't thrust in quickly, like most guys who slept with her did. Oh no, this guy was going for the major climax. He buried himself slowly, inch by glorious inch. It was delicious torture. She trembled. She threw her head from side to side. She couldn't help it; she moaned.

"Yes, my naughty wife. How you love to be punished." Now firmly seated in her vagina, his cock felt huge. Thick and long and absolutely perfect. Tears stung her eyes. Tears from what, she had no idea. No, maybe she did have a little bit of an idea. For some reason, she felt like she'd come home, like she'd found the man she'd been missing for a long, long time.

His withdrawal was just as slow and agonizing as his entry and it did everything to stir her lust to new heights. Whereas with every other man she'd always been after the Big O, with this one she didn't want it to be over. Yet she felt her body racing toward the finish line, without any help from her mind. In fact, she was trying to resist it, yet she couldn't.

Powerless. Completely out of control, of even her own body. And oh, so happy! What was going on?

Was it the ropes? Was it the wicked promises he whispered in her ear as he fell into a slow but steady pattern of thrusts with that wonderful cock of his? Was it the fact that she didn't even know his name?

He leaned lower, until his lightly haired chest brushed against her erect nipples. It tickled and she gasped in surprise. "Yes, that's it, love. Let yourself go. Give it all to me, everything you are, everything you think and feel and need. It's all mine now. You are mine."

Insane or not, at the moment she could think of nothing but being his, in every way. "Oh, God," she heard herself mutter. She tipped her hips to meet his thrusts, deepen them. She loved the way his cock glided in and out, caressing that special spot inside her, the one that sent waves of liquid heat crashing through her body. She blinked open her eyes, not even sure she remembered closing them. Her gaze met his. It was fierce, yet she sensed a tenderness churning below the surface. Hot and demanding, but also kind and loving.

"Who are you?" she asked, letting her eyelids fall closed again. He was too close, it was all too intense. A part of her wanted to hide while another wanted to bare everything, all her fears, disappointments. Doubts.

He stilled for a moment, leaving his cock deep inside her. "I'm anyone you want me to be. Your refuge." He kissed her forehead. "Your protector." He kissed her left eye and then her right. "Your friend." He kissed her chin. "Your Master." He slanted his mouth over hers in a kiss so gentle yet thorough she felt like she'd died and gone to heaven.

When he resumed his steady thrusts, she *knew* she'd died and gone to heaven.

Her climax swept over her like a tsunami, throwing her into a world of pulsing, heated wetness where nothing existed but the man on top of her. She heard him shout his release, felt his cock thicken and his thrusts quicken as he pumped his seed deep inside her.

Afterward, he pulled out, untied her, rolled onto his side and held her sweetly in his arms. He kissed the angry red welts on her wrists then dragged one hand down the length of her hair, plucking up a lock and holding it to his nose to inhale.

"What is this scent? It's so sweet, yet nutty. Is it from that strange world where Brothers Rido and Ikuni found you?"

"Strange world? It's just coconut. And it didn't come from a *world*, it came from a bottle. Suave, as a matter of fact. Hardly something beyond the common American's reach."

"American." He sighed. "I wish you could take me to this

world you visit. I would very much like to see it." He nuzzled her neck, his whiskers stirring up a serious case of goose bumps. "Such smells. I can only imagine what sights you've seen. I talked to the Wise One. He told me about . . . about you. About your world. Tried to explain why you had to leave. I don't understand it all," he growled. "He told me I shouldn't have brought you back. But I couldn't stand it, dammit . . . I missed you. I had to have you back. You are my wife. Mine. He had no right taking you away from me."

Even though Kylie didn't know this guy, she sensed his sadness, his desperation to reach her. Who was his wife? And why had she left? And why did he think she was his wife? And who was this Wise One? And what did she make of all this talk about "her world"? She tipped her head to look at his face. He looked rumpled and adorable and sated. But also sad. Like he'd lost his best friend.

Oh, man.

She had to tell him the truth. Somehow. She was a complete jerk for not driving her point home earlier, instead of allowing him to drive his, quite literally. But now that her hormones were in check, the gag had been loosened from the voice of her conscience. "Listen, we need to talk about this 'wife' thing," she began. Not sure how to continue, she sat up and wrapped a blanket around herself.

He caught her hand in his and gave her a sharp gaze. "I won't let you leave again. No. Tell me I have no right to ask about your leaving, and I will accept it, only because you are our Goddess. But you will always be mine." He dragged his fingers through his hair. The motion set the muscles of his arm and shoulder rippling. It was some sight. "I wish you could talk to me about these things. I . . . I understand why you can't. I've known for a long time there would be a time—I mean, being the Goddess, you are forced to—"

"The goddess?" she repeated, so incredibly lost. Where was this conversation going? He thought she was his wife. He thought she was a goddess? A goddess who had left for some purpose he didn't know and had no right to ask about? This whole thing sounded like the plot of some B-grade sci-fi film. Nervous, she stood, dragging the blanket off the bed.

"What is it? What do you need? I'll call for your maids." The man—her lover, supposed husband, whatever—scrambled over the bed and pulled a cord at the head. It was interesting, how he'd changed since they'd had sex. Before, he'd been so forceful, so sexy and self-assured and strong. Now there was something else there, a little bit of uncertainty, which only added to her confusion. It also made her feel really, really guilty.

She firmed up her resolve and looked him dead in the eye. "Okay. Last time. I'm not your wife. I'm certainly no goddess, unless you're talking about the goddess of disasters, because that I will accept. And I'm extremely sorry for taking advantage of the situation and having sex with you, thereby letting you think I was indeed your wife. Now, if you don't mind, I'm going to head home, have a glass, or two, or maybe a bottle, of wine to help me forget all about this—not that it was all bad, mind you," she said, wanting to spare his male pride. "But I had no right and I'd better go. I need to get ready for Monday." When he didn't say anything, she accepted that as his acceptance that her leaving was best, and headed for the door.

It was unlocked but she didn't step outside. No sooner did she open the door than she halted, agape, and even more confused than she'd been not ten seconds earlier. Standing before her were not one, not two, but three women. Three women with the same blonde hair that wasn't straight or curly. Three women with the same features that weren't ugly but weren't exactly beautiful, either. Three women with the same body, fair-skinned and barely covered in matching outfits that looked like bejeweled bikinis.

They were, in fact, all three mirror images. Exact replicas . . . of herself!

TWO

"WIFE, IF I MUST, I'll tie you to the bed again," came that gravelly male voice from somewhere behind Kylie. "You haven't yet had your punishment. You will not leave me again."

Stunned, she staggered. Her shoulder smacked into the door frame. Her gaze hopped from one shockingly familiar face to the next like a grasshopper on crack. Her three clones eyed her with curiosity for a split second before literally dropping to their knees at her feet.

"What is it you wish of us?" asked Clone Number One, her forehead practically resting on Kylie's big toe.

"We live to serve you," said Clone Number Two.

"Our Goddess," said Clone Number Three. "We did not know you had returned."

"Wife! Return to me," demanded the nearly forgotten man in the room behind her.

Kylie took a moment to steady herself, both literally and figuratively. For some reason, everyone around here—wherever here was, she'd yet to figure that one out—thought she was a goddess. Royalty—no, *deity*. They looked like they were literally worshipping her feet. It was creepy. She'd never been a deity before—at least, not outside her own deluded fantasies.

She glanced down. Three identical faces tipped up for a split second then dropped again. She shuddered. It was seriously weird looking at her own face and body on other people. But at least now she understood why the man inside thought she was his wife.

Well, kind of explained it. Evidently, his wife was the Goddess—goddess with a capital G, gauging by the emphasis they put on the word. And she figured it was a safe assumption that the Goddess was also her mirror image, just like the three girls paying homage to her pedicure. That left only a few niggling questions. First, where had the real Goddess gone? Second, how did she happen to have a tattoo identical to the Goddess's when it was a completely original design? And third, where the heck was she? Some bizarre country in Outer Mongolia?

She decided getting answers from her so-called husband would be her first choice. Going to the one he'd called the Wise One would be a backup, Plan B. "Okay, girls. Off your knees. You're going to get calluses . . . or scabs . . . or something."

The three servants all stood, shrinking from her attempts to touch them, and resumed a "how can we serve you" stance. She had a feeling if she told them to leap off the nearest bridge they'd do it without thinking. That made her feel very odd. Powerful, but also out of sorts.

"At ease, troops," she joked, trying to hide her discomfort. It was going to take some getting used to, speaking to her own face times three. "Don't sweat it. I . . . um, changed my mind." She forced a smile that she didn't exactly feel like producing. "I'll call you if I need anything." She backed into the room. Before she got far enough inside to shut the door, her backside bumped into something hard and warm, with a very curious protuberance at about her lower-back level.

"You're acting very strangely." Behind her, the man set his hands on her shoulders. His fingers worked the muscles of her neck, which suddenly felt like hard, painful lumps.

"Like I said, there is a reason for that." Knowing if she let him continue the shoulder rub, she'd be on the floor playing Hide-the-Protuberance in about three minutes flat, she took a large step forward then turned to face him. Her mouth worked, but nothing came out. Her gaze insisted on dropping to his very impressive cock. She blinked real slow, so that she saw more of the back of her eyelids than the naked man. Still, the words sat in her throat, hung up somewhere between her belly and mouth.

Whew, it would help immensely if he were dressed. And had a hood over his head so she couldn't see his unbelievably handsome face . . .

"What is it?" he asked.

. . . And if he talked through a synthesizer so his voice sounded like Alvin and the Chipmunks. Rodents did not make her wet and dizzy.

"I told you," she said, her eyes closed. "I'm not your wife. Not. Your. Wife. I've never met you." She was on a roll, finally able to speak. Yay! Feeling brave, she opened her eyes and allowed her gaze to settle on his forehead—it was attractive while not being quite so distracting. "I don't even know your name, which I have to admit, is a first for me, since we just"—her gaze decided a forehead was not fertile ground and slid lower, to his full, pouty lower lip"—had the most incredible sex."

He didn't speak for a while, just stood there, head tipped a little, gaze drilling hers. Naked. Naked and yummy and curious. Or maybe intrigued. She couldn't be sure. All she could be sure about was that he liked something he saw, heard, smelled or tasted. The protuberance was still at full staff. Did it ever go down? Had he OD'd on the little blue pill?

"Anyway, if you could," she continued, trying hard not to think too much about the wonder of his never-ending erection. "I want to go home and I was hoping you'd answer some questions for me."

"Perhaps. But you will not leave." He crossed his arms over his scrumptious chest and rested a bulky shoulder against the wall.

Wasn't he going to sit down? Put some clothes on? Do something besides stand there buck naked and field questions like a Major League batter? She'd pitch. He'd swing . . . and score a home run.

She motioned toward a chair and he nodded, walked himself over to said chair and sat. Yes. That was a little better. At least now certain . . . things . . . weren't quite as distracting.

Since when was she so enamored by the sight of an erect penis?

She cleared her throat. "First, your name? Could you please tell me your name?"

"Xur, but you should know—"

"Okay. Good. Xur." At least now she could say she knew his name. First name only. But it was a start. Beggars couldn't be choosers. She'd get the nitty-gritty later . . . maybe . . . hopefully. "And what city are we in?"

"The city of Celestine."

"Celestine?" She rummaged around her brain, trying to recall where, if anywhere, she might have heard the name. Didn't strike her as familiar. Not at all. "I'm not the best at geography. Flunked every test in high school. Uh, could you tell me what state that's in? Are we still in Michigan? Maybe in the Upper Peninsula?"

His eyebrows bunched together. "I haven't heard of this place, Michigan."

"Haven't heard of Michigan? Have you heard of North America?"

"North Ameri—? What?" he asked, looking like she'd just spoken to him in Swahili.

"The continent. North America," she said, enunciating.

"Huh?" He gave her a blank stare.

"Earth?" she tried desperately. Surely he knew Earth. They were on Earth! There wasn't such a thing as life on other planets. Or space travel.

"Earth?" he repeated, like it was the most foreign word he'd ever heard.

"Yes, Earth. Please. Tell me you have heard of Earth? Blue planet with cute white fluffy clouds. Third from the sun . . . or is it the fourth? I can never remember."

"Perhaps a visit to the Wise One would help," he suggested, standing.

Time for Plan B. She so didn't want to think about the possibility of missing work on Monday. What would Mr. Baudeur say? "Yes. Oh, yes. Let's go see the Wise One."

He beat her to the door, opened it and motioned for her to precede him. She paused. "Aren't you going to put on some clothes first?"

"Clothes?" He gave her another confused stare. Then he laughed. Oh, what shudders and shivers his rumbly chuckle birthed in her body. "How you delight me, wife. I'm so glad to have you back. Come, let's go speak with the Wise One. He'll help us both understand what's happened."

Eager to find out what planet she was on—she could think of very few places on Earth where men walked around stark nekkid in the streets in broad daylight, glory as it was—she hurried through the door and out into an expansive corridor that reminded her of a castle, or even the Catholic church her grandmother used to take her to when she was a kid. The beams on the ceiling reminded her of a whale's ribs, arching up to the center and meeting the spine that ran down the length. The walls looked like they were carved out of solid rock. Rough. Damp, she realized when she let her fingertips trail along as she walked. The air was damp, too, and smelled salty, like the sea.

After following Xur a mile or two—or so it felt—they entered a huge room filled with people. Immediately she noticed a couple things. First, every woman in the place had her face, which was, like, weirder than her strangest dream ever! And every male was completely nude and sporting a hard-on.

Was this heaven or hell? How would a girl know?

When she took her first step into the room, everyone, man, woman and child, dropped to their knees and lowered their heads in homage.

Oh my God, it was strange.

She wrapped the blanket tighter around herself, not that she had anything to hide. Now that she thought about it, every woman in the place had her lumpy butt with a touch of stubborn cellulite. And every man in the place had seen it.

Gag! She tugged the blanket tighter.

"This way," Xur said. He took her hand. The touch gave her just the slightest sense of comfort. This was a strange, strange place. Shocking in so many ways, she was afraid to turn the next corner. At least with him at her side she didn't feel quite so alone.

She tipped her head to deliver a smile of appreciation his way. He deserved it.

He shot one back at her, although his wasn't exactly an innocent "you're welcome" type of expression. More like "you're welcome, now let's go back and get busy."

"Only a little further." He pushed open a huge door at the far end of the room and they stepped into yet another corridor. This one was, thankfully, much shorter. It led to a small, intimate room filled from floor to ceiling with books.

A young man sat at a desk, his head lowered over the thin, dusty pages of some enormous book.

"Wise One," Xur said, following Kylie into the room and closing the door behind him.

The young guy—who kind of resembled Kylie's mental picture of a surfer dude, long, shaggy blond hair streaked by the sun, tan skin—lifted his head and gave her a smile. She half expected him to greet Xur with a Southern Californian "Dude."

"The Goddess. It's good to see you. But I told you"—the yet-to-be-proven Wise One gave Xur a glare—"it's too soon. It isn't safe for her to return. What have you done?" The wise guy rounded the huge desk. Kylie was relieved to see he was wearing a little white wrappy thing around his hips, hiding his privates. As it was, she wasn't buying the whole Wise One thing. With his danglies hanging out in the breeze, she'd have an even harder time taking him seriously. Funny, she had no problems taking Xur seriously, dangly parts notwithstanding. "Leave us," he demanded, directing his command at Xur.

Xur didn't take the order too well. Clearly a man who was used to making demands, not abiding by them, he visibly gritted his teeth and glared at the Wise One. There was this little testosterone vibe, a silent pissing match. Xur didn't exactly lose, but he was the bigger man and accepted the fact that he had to leave. Kylie's respect for him swelled.

The second the door closed behind him, the Wise One/surfer

dude said, "Shit, I was hoping he wouldn't go dragging you back yet. I told those two assholes they could check up on you but couldn't touch you. Fucking dicks."

"Mind telling me what's going on? That man out there says I'm his wife but I sure as heck don't remember being married. And what's with the Goddess stuff? And while we're at it, why are there a bunch of women out there who look exactly like me? I mean, this whole thing is just plain scary!"

"Here's the score," the Wise One said, plopping his white-wrapped butt on the desk. "Yes, you're married to Xur. You're the Goddess, you just don't remember, and we're both from the same place, you and me—Plymouth, Michigan. We went to school together, good old Pioneer Middle School. I'm sure you don't remember me . . ."

Where was this conversation going? She was married? Huh?

"Anyway, I always had this thing for you—thought you were hot. And I was working on this secret project for the government that I can't talk about when I discovered a portal to this . . . dimension or whatever you want to call it. Don't ask me to explain it again, because I've tried. You didn't get it. Anyway, the people here had some problems with . . . procreating, to put it politely. And well, the men needed women, vessels so to speak."

"Vessels for what?"

He gave her a guilty smile. "I had you cloned. Don't ask me how I got your DNA, 'cause I've tried to explain that, too. And I can't explain how your clones are all the same age as you are. Suffice it to say certain functions of life move at different speeds if I manipulate the portal, so your clones could leave Plymouth, Michigan, as infants yet enter Celestine as adults—"

Her head was spinning. Portals? Clones? Time warps? "Um—"

"Okay. Won't go there again, either. Yeah. Anyway, thanks to me, there are like hundreds of Kylie Mannings here. And you're the Goddess because, well, because I said so."

"So, if I'm the Goddess of this place, why don't I remember anything?"

"Because there's this group of people who aren't exactly happy with the arrangements here. Motherfuckers want you dead." He cleared his throat. "So, I sent you back to Plymouth, hoping you'd be safe there for the time being. Oh, and I had your memories erased. You know, for your protection."

"How very thoughtful."

"Hey, I tried." He didn't look the least bit apologetic, even though from the sound of it, he'd manipulated her life big-time, ferrying her back and forth between "dimensions," stealing her DNA, creating hundreds of copies of her . . . "Until you were sent back, you were quite happy with things here."

"Yes, well, I'm not sure what I feel right now," she said truthfully. None of it made any sense. Dimensions. Clones. People after her. Memories erased. There wasn't a bit of believability in any of it! Had she fallen asleep with the Sci Fi Channel on again? After a fierce pinch to her thigh failed to wake her up, she figured she had no choice but to go with the flow for now. If this was indeed a dream, she couldn't really be hurt or killed. Right? "Assuming you're telling me the truth, how long was I gone?"

"Oh, I'm telling you the truth all right. Time here moves at a different rate than back in Plymouth. Days on this side, years on yours." He cleared his throat. "So, now that we've had our little chat, I hope you're feeling better."

"Not really."

"Sorry. If it makes things any easier, the memories will come back. Over time."

"Time? I don't have time. I want to go home. My new job starts—"

"Not possible. At least not right now. I don't have the ability to open the portal yet—transporting three people at once drained the power supply—so you're going to have to hang low for a few, at least until it recharges."

"But my job—"

"Nothing I can do about it. Sorry. Now listen carefully. Until I can get these assholes taken care of, you'll just have to sit tight, stay out of sight. Don't worry. The leader's as good as dead. I know who he is. Just gotta find where he's hiding. Here's a thought, how about taking a second honeymoon? You can get reacquainted with that husband of yours." He winked.

Her head swam. Too much information. *Can't go home? Her job. A husband? A honeymoon? Someone wanted her dead? A husband?* Her cheeks heated. "He's really my husband? You're sure?"

"Positive. It's all legal and everything. I have proof," he said, hurrying back around the desk.

"No, no. That's okay. Call me crazy, but for some reason I believe you. But I have a question. Why do people want me dead?"

Now he looked guilty. He shifted nervously in his seat. His gaze dropped to the desktop. "It's sort of complicated."

"Try me."

"I guess you could call it professional jealousy. With my help, you sort of displaced someone else as reigning Goddess."

Finally, some hope of things returning to the "normal" she remembered. The life back in Michigan. The job she'd busted her ass to get. "No biggie. There we go! A solution. Tell the former Goddess she can have her goddessness back. No hard feelings. And I'll go back to Plymouth and live the life I *remember,* just like I want to. It's a win-win situation, except for maybe you—"

He shook his head. "It's not that simple. You see, the only way a Goddess can be removed from her throne is by death."

She swallowed a boulder-sized lump in her throat. "You mean you killed her? For me? I didn't ask you to do that!"

"No, you didn't *ask, you* killed her."

"Huh?" That lump swelled to the size of a semi truck. "No way! I'm not a killer. I don't kill people. Heck, I don't kill insects." She fanned her flaming face. Just the thought of her killing someone was shocking. He couldn't make her believe she killed someone. No, no, no! A lie. It had to be a lie!

"It was an accident, when you came out of the portal."

An accident! Okay, that she could accept a little better. She'd killed the Goddess. Kind of like Dorothy killed the witch in *The Wizard of Oz*. "So, if it was an accident, why are these people so hell-bent on revenge?"

He shrugged. "Because that's the way of this place. A life for a life."

She was so not liking this place! Then something he said earlier played back through her mind. Life for a life? "These people kill anyone who kills, regardless of whether it's by accident or not. And you're going to kill their leader?"

"I have no choice. With him gone, the others should surrender."

She didn't need any crystal ball to see trouble was brewing. For both of them, Goddess and Wise One. "I don't like this. Send me back to Plymouth. Send me back now."

"I told you, I can't. Not until the solar cells recharge. In case you haven't noticed, this place isn't exactly the most technologically advanced culture in the universe. Can't even get a pack of AA batteries when you need them. You're stuck here for now.

And you're in danger. So, before they find you, you need to hustle out of here. Word has spread already. Several people know you've returned."

"Shit, shit, shit! I don't like this at all. I have no control. None whatsoever. I have one last question."

"Shoot."

"I gotta know, what did you get out of all this? Why'd you do it in the first place?"

"Why?" He sat, kicked his feet on the desk and flashed a Cheshire cat smile. "I was merely a man in Detroit, Michigan. Here, I'm practically a god. The revered Wise One. With an abundance of very willing you-clones. Simply put, I'm in heaven."

Kylie shuddered. Too much information there, too.

"Now, go, hide. Do the Goddess thing. I'll send word when it's safe to return to the palace. In the meantime, I'll tell that husband of yours where I want you hidden—and I know he'll take matters into his own hands if you refuse to cooperate." The slimy smile he gave her made her want to puke, even though she had a notion that any discipline Xur decided to dole out would be more pleasure than punishment.

THREE

KYLIE HAD TO GIVE IT TO the Wise One, his idea of an appropriate hiding place for a Goddess was first-rate. Not quite the Fairmont, but the so-called cottage was not only huge but also incredibly beautiful, with a lush flower garden surrounding the entry. The sweet scents of lavender and roses filled her nostrils as she followed Xur into the mammoth building through a door tall enough and wide enough to fit an elephant. An armed guard stood beside the door, motionless, like a statue, a toy. He didn't even blink.

The second Kylie stepped inside, she grew breathless again. They stood inside a giant hallway with high ceilings and rich fabrics draped over the walls. Rich red. Deep purple. It made the place look like a medieval New Orleans bordello, but classier. Kylie had the urge to sing "Lady Marmalade." *Voulez-vous coucher avec moi ce soir*. Dressed in a bejeweled bikini like her maids had been wearing back at the palace, and following a man who was still completely nude, with an adorable butt—she'd noticed *that* quite some time ago—she felt saucy, a little reckless and wild. The journey to their hiding place—made on foot!—had taken quite a while, many hours. She'd played the role of servant to Xur, while strategically hiding her tattoo with a white cape that hung from her shoulders. The long walk had given her a chance to sort out the information the Wise Ass had dumped on her.

Wise One, her butt! Yes, she was steamed! He'd effed her life, dragging her through portals, making a bazillion clones without her permission, erasing her memory, risking her new job! And why? So he could fuck her a million times over! She couldn't wait to get the hell out of this place. Men!

It was a good thing she was outside reaching distance. Given the opportunity, there was no saying what she might do to him.

But she had to admit, despite being outraged, there was a part of her that was appreciating the finer aspects of being a goddess with a capital G for a day or two, particularly where it came to her chosen husband. Despite the fact that she had no recollection of marrying the man, there was something between them, a current of energy that sizzled in the air when they were near each other, as well as a sense of comfort and trust. It was a very strange thing for her, to trust a man she really didn't know. In the normal world, she didn't trust men at all, even the ones she knew very well.

They filled the hours walking, engaged in friendly chatter. Xur Phoenix—she finally knew his last name!—was trying hard to help her remember him, their life together in Celestine. And make her forget the one she had back in Plymouth. It almost made her feel guilty that she couldn't.

"A bath?" Xur asked, leading her through a series of smaller hallways into a gorgeous room also swathed in heavy fabrics and sporting what had to be the world's largest bed dead in the center of the floor. "Or food first?" He took both her hands in his and pulled her toward the bed, dusting each of her fingertips with a little kiss. "Mmmm. You must be starved. I'll ring for food." He reached for a cord at the head of the bed.

Kylie's stomach rumbled, casting its vote. "Sure. Okay. Maybe

I could take a bath while we're waiting?" A knock sounded at the door. "Already? Wow! What service."

Minutes later she was nude, soaking in a steamy tub full of scented water and munching on sweet, juicy fruits and admiring her husband's finer assets. She even let herself forget about her job for a while. Surely, once her boss discovered she was missing, he wouldn't hold missing a day or two of work against her. Being kidnapped couldn't be cause for dismissal.

Maybe she wouldn't kill old Wise Butt after all. When the aches in her legs and feet had faded, the rumbling hunger in her belly sated and the bathwater tepid, she stepped out, accepting a towel from a Kylie clone. Her skin tingled as she toweled off. The whole time she'd been bathing, there'd been the sense of expectancy. Xur had sat patiently, not rushing her, but there was something in his eyes, a hunger she hadn't been able to ignore. It made him look fierce, like an animal. She practically expected him to pounce on her the moment she was out of the water. The anticipation made her shiver.

"Are you chilled?" He looked worried. That made her feel all soft and girly inside. He genuinely cared about her.

"Oh, no. Not at all." She stood, cold water still dribbling from her wet hair, about ten feet from him and the bed. That was a big bed all right. And a big man. Big, hard cock, too. She shivered again, not because she was scared or cold. There was nothing to be scared of. Nothing at all. And she sure wasn't cold. In fact, her pussy was tingly. Warm, moist and getting hotter by the second. So was the rest of her.

He closed the distance between them, took her hand and led her to the bed. "Come. I'll keep you warm." The suggestion in his voice told her the double entendre was intentional.

She didn't resist. What woman could? He lay on the bed and

pulled her on top of him. But before she could get comfy, he did a logroll, landing her flat on her back with him on top. His face hovered over hers. His panting breaths warmed her cheeks. His fiery gaze warmed her other parts. She squirmed underneath him. There were some parts that burned to be touched and she was determined to put them in contact with him one way or another.

"Goddess help me, but I can't resist you. I know you have no memory of me, and I'm trying to be patient, but I can't help myself. I want to fuck you."

"To hell with patience. I want you to fuck me, too."

He grinned, licked his lips and she watched, recalling what that tongue had done to her body, her nipples, her pussy earlier. "You know, I haven't yet punished you for leaving."

"Hey, according to your Wise One that wasn't my fault."

He caught both her hands in his and pinned them over her head. "I know that now," he said, his lips brushing over hers as he spoke. "But I figured I wouldn't hold it against you, since you're so fond of being disciplined."

This time the shiver was more like a shudder. Head to toe, she quaked. A wash of heat cascaded down her body, churning between her legs.

"Uh—"

He pressed his mouth to hers, kissing her breath away. His tongue slipped between her parted lips, probing her mouth while he gathered her wrists in one hand and used the other to explore parts of her anatomy that were quite pleased to have a visitor. He rolled her nipple between his thumb and forefinger. It was glorious agony. Little blades of pleasure-pain razored out from her nipple, skittering along her spine. Her pussy clenched around its own emptiness. She rocked her pelvis back and forth against him, trying to grind away the ache growing between her legs.

He broke the kiss and trailed little nips and licks along one side of her neck. Dying to drag her fingertips down his bare chest, to feel the crisp hair sprinkled over satin-soft skin, she wriggled her hands, struggling to break free from his grip.

"Oh, no you don't." He tightened his grip on her wrists until she yelped, then loosened it only slightly. "You may be the Goddess, but in private, I'm the Master." He sat up, left her for a moment.

Dazed and feeling alone, she rolled onto her side and watched him as he walked to an armoire and opened the doors. She could see inside, lots of leather strappy-looking things. Floggers maybe? Leather bindings? He returned to her with armfuls of stuff. His face flushed, his cock at full staff—and looking quite scrumptious, she could add—he dropped the goodies on the bed and flashed her a grin that made her heart hop in her chest. She sat up to inspect what he'd brought over, but he gave her a stern shake of the head and pointed at the mattress.

"Lie down," he demanded.

Turned on by the sharp tone of his voice, she gladly flopped back onto the bed. This incredibly sexy, strong man was her husband. Husband! The mind boggled. She felt like she was sleeping with both a stranger and an old friend at the same time. On one hand, she didn't know what he'd do next, which made her jumpy and jittery. On the other, she was so comfortable with him, she wasn't afraid to explore, to have fun, to give in to the hunger building up inside her. She felt so free, so happy, so . . . alive!

"Over on your stomach," Xur demanded, his voice dripping with sexual promise.

Trembling, dizzy with the need for release, she complied.

He grabbed her ankles and pulled, dragging her across the bed until her hips were at the edge of the mattress and her feet were on the floor. Her barely covered ass was up there, front and center. And she was one very happy Goddess.

"I haven't spanked you in a long time," he said, grazing her shoulders with something soft and tickly. She fought back a shiver. "Would you like me to spank you?"

"Oh . . ."

"Is that a yes?" He dragged whatever it was he had up around the back of her neck, then down her spine to her bottom.

This time she couldn't help shuddering. "Yes," she squeaked.

"Mmmm." He lifted the toy away. "Have you forgotten how to address me?"

"Uh . . . yes, please?" she offered, not sure what he meant.

He tsked her and pressed his hot, yummy bod against her back. His erect cock poked at the material barely covering her ass. He whispered in her ear, "I will remind you only once more. Master. I am your Master when we are in our bed."

"Yes. Of course. You did say that, didn't you. Sorry . . . er, Master." This "Master" thing was new and strange to her, but oh, so much fun! She'd never ever role-played in bed but she'd always wanted to try. Yay, this was going to be great! She could literally feel the pulse of blood rushing to her pussy. Her heart was pounding against her ribs like a jackhammer. She was giddy and dizzy and squirmy. So hot. So, so hot.

"Much better." His voice was low and rumbly, like a bear. She really liked the way it sounded. It made her feel safe and happy and sexy. "If anything hurts too much, or you want me to stop, say . . . Michigan."

"Michigan?"

"Yes, Michigan," Xur repeated. Standing behind her with Kylie draped over the edge of the mattress, her rear end facing him, he pulled her towel down, down, down. Off her bottom, down her trembling legs. He left it on the floor at her feet.

"Ohhhhh. Okay," she said breathlessly. Every part of her body tingled with pent-up sensual energy. The anticipation of being spanked was like a drug, so intense, so exquisite. Her heart was knocking against her rib cage like a fist. Her head was swimmy and foggy. Her nerves tight and jittery. She hadn't known it would be like this. Had never guessed.

She heard the light *whap* of leather striking skin before she felt the sting of the impact. Caught her by surprise. She jumped, gasped and fisted the coverlet. The skin of her buttocks stung good. It was the most magnificent pain. The second one landed in a different spot, warming the skin there. And the third struck lower. Her fanny was on fire—in a wonderful way. Her whole body was sizzling with erotic energy. Her knees were wobbly. She pulled on the coverlet, worried she'd sink to the floor.

Being the gentleman he clearly was, Xur didn't let her fall. He kissed her stinging skin then helped her up onto the bed and onto her back. His expression was tight, jaw rigid, as he looked down on her, his eyes full of raw wanting. He ran his hands down her torso, following the motion with his eyes. The way he looked at her, like she was the most beautiful, sexiest woman in the universe. Like he could hardly contain his need for her for another second. It made her body ache everywhere. In a very good way. Before she could beg for relief from the agony he was stirring in her body, he kneeled over her, settled his hips between her legs and thrust his cock deep inside.

The air escaped her lungs in a quick whoosh. At precisely the same time, her body launched like a rocket toward climax. His quick rhythmic thrusts were exactly what her body craved. Muscles coiled tight. Heat surging through her veins. As if he knew instinctively what she needed, he shifted his weight, sitting up until her entire body was uncovered. He pushed her knees apart and back and drew rapid circles over her clit.

He stopped a bazillionth of a second before she reached orgasm. Pulled that yummy cock out of her pussy. Quit stroking her clit. "No!" Only one more thrust of his cock would've done it. Sent her to that happy place where sensations blurred together and nothing but pulsing bliss existed. Not even a full thrust would've been needed. A half stroke. A twitch might've even done it for her. She wanted to scream, the frustration was so intense. She tipped her hips, desperately hoping he'd get the hint. "Not more punishment. Please, no more."

"Oh no, my Goddess. I'm not punishing you now," he said, laughter lifting his voice. He sounded too cheerful for her. Way too damn cheerful. What was he so freaking happy about? "I'm rewarding you."

Rewards were good reasons to be happy, though she wasn't exactly feeling rewarded at the moment. "Reward?"

"Oh, yes. Reward." He motioned toward the forgotten collection of goodies he'd brought over from the armoire. "We can't let all this stuff just sit here unused, can we?"

"Oh. No. I suppose not." She glanced at the pile of sex toys. Outside of a plastic vibrator, she had no idea what those thingies were. Lots of chrome-plated doohickeys. And black leather. Mmmm. Her internal generator was revving up again, creating a whole lot of heat.

"On your knees," he commanded, as he scooped up a small white cardboard box. Looked a lot like the kind of jewelry box you might get with the purchase of some junk jewelry from a discount store.

Curious, a little wobbly, and really, really warm, Kylie forced herself upright, on her knees on the mattress. Between her near-boneless state and the mattress's shifting as Xur moved, it was no small feat holding her position.

"Very nice," he practically purred. He flipped the top off the box and pulled out a narrow silver chain. Or rather, what looked like three chains fastened together. A small alligator clamp hung from the end of each one. The little grippy parts were covered with what looked like black rubber.

What the heck was it?

He held two of the little clips in his hands and stared hungrily at a point about eight inches or so south of her chin. Didn't take her long to figure out where those to clamps were headed. But what about the third one?

Just because he had to figure it would nearly kill her, he bent his head and swirled his tongue around each nipple. They stood out, erect and sensitized. Then he clipped the ends of the chains first to one, then the other.

Oh, God! The sweet agony! It pinched just enough to feel really, really good.

"How're you liking your reward so far?" He smiled at her with such an evil fire in his eye, she thought she might melt.

"Good," she squeaked. She sucked in a gasp when he tugged gently on the chain. Oh, he was a mean, mean man! Mean in such a very nice way. Still had no idea where that third clamp went.

Still holding the one loose end of the chain, he rolled onto his back. "Straddle my face. I want to eat you."

The promise heavy in those words made her whimper. And

the little yank he gave the chain made her do more than that. She shuddered, crawled on hands and knees until her pussy was positioned over his mouth. She heard him audibly inhale.

"You smell so good." His voice was husky. Ubermale. Sensuous. He reached up and gripped her hips. His fingertips dug into the soft flesh. He pulled down until she was literally sitting on his face. His nose rubbed up against her pubic bone. His lips, tongue and teeth performed magic on her clit.

Her legs were trembling. She bent over at the waist and supported her upper body with her outstretched arms. "Oh. My. God." She felt the bite of the little clamp on her clit. Her eyeballs bulged. She could feel them. She straightened up and the chains connecting her nipples and clit pulled against one another, tugging simultaneously on all three places. Minibolts of pleasure-pain arced through her body like zaps of electricity. She gasped. "Xur!" Afraid to move, afraid the amazing sensations would become too intense, she froze in position, her pussy hovering over his face. Her shoulders hunched down a bit to keep the chains from pulling too hard.

"Shoulders back," he demanded. "It'll feel so much better that way."

"Oh God, oh God, oh God!" She slowly pushed her shoulders back. The chains tightened again, pulling at her nipples and clit. Another series of hot, intense bursts of pleasure shot through her body.

Then he stared fucking her pussy with his tongue and those short, staccato surges lengthened and smoothed out into long, languid waves.

While he fucked her pussy with his tongue, she slowly rocked her hips, intentionally increasing and decreasing the pull on the clamps. Such sweet agony! Like nothing she'd ever felt before.

She wanted to come but at the same time wanted the tension coiling tight inside her to keep building, building, building until she couldn't stand it anymore. She knew the choice was not hers to make. Xur would decide. That realization made her even hotter. Even more desperate for release.

He lifted her hips, and holding her up, slid out from under her. She didn't object, knowing in her heart that whatever he had planned next would be even better. "Down on your hands and knees."

Yes, oh yes. She loved being fucked doggy-style. Quivered with delight when he scooted around her back end on his knees and took her hips in his hands again.

The mattress shifted as he reached to the side for something. A soft click and hum told her what it was before she felt the cool plastic tip probing the cleft between her ass cheeks. It was not quite in the right place . . .

"Lower," she whispered. She lifted her fanny, hoping to guide the vibrator closer to her pussy.

"No. That's not where I'm aiming."

A gulp of air lodged itself in her throat. Nothing as large as a vibrator had ever been in her ass. Anal beads, yes. The little teeny, tiny beads. A fingertip. That too. But not a dildo. Or a cock. And at the moment, she wasn't sure if she wanted to keep it that way or not.

She felt him spreading something cool and wet around her anus. It dribbled down toward her pussy and she reflexively clenched her inner muscles, curled her back and tucked her bottom down. The soft buzzing vibrations hummed around her hole. That felt good. Better than good. She wondered what it would feel like to have those yummy pulses inside her ass while he fucked her pussy.

Maybe she had been a little hasty about the vibrator?

"I know how much you love this."

"I do?" Had she . . . had he . . . ? She wished her memory would come back.

"Oh yes, especially this part. When I enter you oh, so slowly," he murmured in a low, silky voice that made her think of decadent chocolate. Smooth and rich and yummy. He pushed a little harder and the very tip of the vibrator slipped inside her anus. The buzzing flowed over her skin, penetrated inside to create the most amazing, sensual sensation.

So close. So close to orgasm her body was tight like overstretched rubber bands. Ready to snap. To explode.

He eased the vibrator deeper inside. So good. So fucking good she couldn't breathe. Her arms shook. Her chest fell to the bed. She didn't care that her face was buried in blankets.

Then he thrust his cock inside her pussy. It was so intense. Buzzing vibrations in her ass. Thick cock in her pussy. She arched her spine and tossed her head backward. The clamps pulled at her nipples, her clit, sending jagged, glorious pulses of pleasure up and down her spine. She heard herself screaming. Heard the *slap, slap, slap* of his thighs striking her fanny as he fell into a steady rhythm. But all that mattered was the vibration deep inside and the intimate strokes of his cock.

Her orgasm washed over her like a hot wave. *Whoosh,* up her body. She relished every moment, measured in loud, thudding heartbeats. And she rejoiced when Xur shouted his release and slowed his thrusts to deep, penetrating movements that drove his cock and seed up against her womb.

Slick with sweat, he dropped onto the mattress. His breathing was ragged and fast. She closed her eyes, turned onto her side, wrapped her arms around his neck and held him, loving the weight of him, the warmth when he logrolled her onto her back.

Pushing up on outstretched arms, he kissed her nose. Her forehead. Her chin. Then he gently removed the vibrator and the delicate chains and clamps and set them aside.

"My Goddess. My life. I have nothing if I don't have you." He combed his fingers through her hair.

She closed her eyes and smiled, inhaling deeply, drawing in the musky-sweet scent of man and sex. "And I . . . I . . . Oh my God." For the first time in her life, she knew. This was the man for her, the one who made her whole. An image flashed through her mind, a memory. Of them together, like this, holding each other after having made love. Of Xur stroking her hair and promising he would never leave her side. He'd love and protect her forever.

She remembered!

It wasn't a lifetime of memories, no. Just a single blip. A moment. Whatever. But she remembered something. Something important and special and wonderful. She remembered how loved she'd felt then. How cherished and contented and whole Xur had made her. That was all she ever needed to remember. If nothing else came back, she didn't care. Xur loved her. Xur cherished her. He was strong yet gentle. He had earned her trust and had possessed her heart. And she was the luckiest damned Goddess in the universe.

So happy, contented, she could weep, she let herself relax, just enjoy the simple pleasure of being held.

But her peace was interrupted by a loud crash, and then shouting. Xur jerked on top of her before rolling off and jumping to his feet.

A man she knew, a man she'd slept with, burst into the room, arm raised, a knife in his fist. He charged at the bed, bloodlust in his eyes.

"Adam?" she murmured.

"Sorry, but it's our way," Adam said. "I tried to convince you to marry me, back in that other world, that place called Michigan. But you refused. All I wanted was to be husband to the Goddess. But you couldn't be bothered. And you didn't have the decency to stay in Michigan so a new Goddess could be selected. Now you must die."

FOUR

THERE WERE A LOT OF things about the past twenty-four hours that had taken Kylie Mannings by surprise. A kidnapping. Learning she was a Goddess. Discovering she lived in an alternate dimension where all the women were her mirror image. Finding out she had a husband.

The shocking nature of all those discoveries paled in comparison to learning her ex-boyfriend wanted her dead. In her life she'd had some ugly breakups, but this one took the cake—the whole bakery, in fact!

While she sat naked on the bed, gaping in silent horror, her husband did the hero thing and charged into action. He literally threw himself at Adam. Adam was ready for him, though, and was able to dodge him much too easily for Kylie's comfort. That knife raised in the air, cold determination on his face, he ran at Kylie like a butcher after a runaway hen. As any sane woman would do, she ran. Of course, she couldn't go far, since the one and only exit was behind him.

Luckily, before Adam caught her, Xur tackled Adam from behind and knocked him to the ground. There was much scuffling and grunting. Male arms and legs swinging. Kylie inched her way around the wrestling men, hoping to make it to the door where she could call for help. As was her luck, she didn't make it. A hand closed around her ankle, snapped around it like a sprung trap. It took her by surprise, as she was moving pretty fast, and made her lose her balance. Before she knew it, she too was in the midst of the melee, pushing, shoving, struggling to break free. She held her own—a feat, considering she'd never thrown a punch in her life. At one point she even managed to break free altogether. She scrambled on all fours from Adam. But seconds later he had her again.

Not once, not twice, but three times something belted her hard, on the back. The pain was unbelievable. It felt like she'd been clobbered with a huge metal club. Within minutes she felt herself getting tired. Bone weary. Heard Xur's voice, but she was too exhausted to struggle anymore. She wanted to go to him but she needed to rest. Her eyelids fell shut and the world faded away. It was so unfair! She'd finally found him again, and now he was lost.

Her husband. Her Master.

XUR BRUTALLY YANKED THE blade out of the man's chest and threw it across the room. He dropped to his knees at Kylie's side.

Was she . . . ?

"Oh, Goddess!" he murmured.

She was so still. Dark blood oozed from the three wounds on her back. The ugly marks marred her smooth, perfect skin and stirred rage anew. His hands shook, his whole body trembled with a bitter mixture of anger and dread.

He glared for a split second at the bastard who lay about ten feet away, eyes wide open in a death stare. He got what he deserved. How dare he attack the beloved Goddess!

His anger cooling, his fears and sorrow swelling in its place, Xur covered his own face, dropped his head and pressed an ear to her back. Would he hear the soft whoosh of air entering her lungs? Or would he hear dead silence?

He held his breath and waited, every muscle in his body trembling.

Nothing. He heard nothing!

"No," he heard himself say. Hot tears streamed from his eyes. This was his fault! If only he'd left her where she was, in that strange world she'd called Michigan. She would've been safe there. His fault. Why, oh why, hadn't he listened? The Wise One had warned him. Now the woman he loved more than life itself was . . . was . . .

He heard something! The softest, most wonderful sound. Air passing to her lungs.

"Praise the Goddess!" She was breathing, but barely. He carefully rolled her over and looked at her face.

Her face was so pale, her lips white. He shouted his relief and jumped to his feet. Help. He needed help. Now. He couldn't let his Goddess die, his life. His love. He shouted as he ran out into the hall. A healer. He needed a healer. Immediately. He would never again doubt the words of the Wise One. And he would never again take the dangers of being the Goddess for granted. If she lived, he would protect her with his very life . . . he would send her back to Michigan, if that was what it took.

He would live without her, if it meant she would be safe and happy. That was all he wished for. He wished for her to be safe and happy.

Since she'd returned, he'd been trying to ignore the obvious—she didn't belong to his world anymore. She didn't belong to him. No man could possess a Goddess.

* * *

THE ALARM WRENCHED KYLIE from her dreamless sleep. Her head buried under pillows, she thrust a hand out and blindly smacked at the air, aiming for the snooze button. On the fifth try, she hit it. The obnoxious buzz ceased and she tried to slip back to sleep for another nine glorious minutes.

Unfortunately, even though her body wanted at least another hour of sleep, her mind wouldn't let her have another minute. She stared at the clock. It was 7:02. More importantly, she was at home. In her house. Lying in her bed. Staring at her alarm clock.

Had that whole clone/alternate-dimension thing been a dream? Had to be.

"Oh, man!" She flung her arm at the nightstand and picked up her cell phone. What day was it? Was it Sunday? Monday? Her back ached. Her muscles were stiff, sore. Had she been sick? Or hurt? The dream had been so vivid, just like the dreams she tended to have when she was ill.

Sunday. It was Sunday. What a relief! At least she wouldn't have to rush to get ready for work. She could just stay in bed, rest. Yes, oh yes. That sounded wonderful. Her back was so sore. What had happened? Did those teenage trick-or-treaters attack her?

She sat up and tried to stretch. Man, what'd they do to her? Beat her up and leave her for dead? How'd she get into bed? She noticed she was nude and shuddered. Had they . . . raped her? She pulled the sheet around herself and glanced at the window. The drapes were partially parted in the center, letting a couple of inches of bright sunlight into the room.

It was so quiet. She felt so alone, and for once being alone didn't feel all that great. Maybe her imaginary husband, Xur, had been a dream, but—God help her—she missed him. Was that possible? To miss someone who didn't exist?

And another thing, she missed who she was when she had been with him, too. In her dream, he'd pulled something out of her somehow, a smidge of recklessness, a hunger for life.

Alone. She was alone. Awake. Xur was gone. Didn't exist. Ugh.

She rolled onto her belly and covered her head with a pillow. Maybe if she fell back asleep, she'd resume the dream. She'd done that once or twice in her life. It might happen. She closed her eyes and concentrated on visualizing Xur's adorable face. His dark eyes and hair. The cute cleft in his chin. "Come on, dream. Come back to me."

Despite the fact that most sound and light were snuffed out by feathers wrapped in 800-thread-count cotton, and she was concentrating on reviving a dream that was fading fast from her memory, she heard the knock on her front door. The hairs on her nape tickled. Who could be here this early on a Sunday morning? Was she imagining things? She jerked, throwing the pillow off, and listened. Yes, there was a knock. A loud, urgent pounding.

She jumped into a pair of sweats and a sweatshirt then hurried down to answer the door.

She peered through the peephole. It couldn't be! Could it? Was that man, dressed head-to-toe in police regalia, Xur? Impossible!

She unlocked the door and swung it open. "Wha—!" Her heart jumped around in her chest like an overwound toy. Her eyes burned. "It's . . . you're real?" she whispered, afraid she'd dozed off and her own voice might wake her up any minute. And then she'd discover he was gone again, a figment of her overactive imagination.

"I found you! Thank the Goddess. I was afraid I wouldn't be able to." He was grinning literally ear-to-ear. "Can I come in?"

"Tell me I'm not dreaming." She staggered backward until her backside hit the sofa table.

"You're not dreaming." He shut the door then closed the distance between them in one long stride. A cloud of coconut-scented air followed him.

Pinching herself, Kylie sniffed the air. She threw her arms around his neck and pressed her cheek to his chest. Real. He was real! He was there. With her. "How? What's going on? And why do you smell like coconuts? I thought you were gone forever. I thought I'd never see you again."

"I found the Suave scented liquid. I like it." His eyes glittered. His hands were restless on her back, wandering up and down.

"I see that." She giggled, couldn't help it. She pulled out of his embrace for a second, just to get a good look at him again. The man was macho beyond compare but smelled like he'd bathed in coconut-scented suntan lotion. Adorable. He was so adorable. And sexy. And real! Her heart felt like it had swelled to ten times its normal size. "But how'd you . . . was that whole Celestine thing a dream? I'm so confused."

He gently led her to the couch, sat next to her and glued his big brown eyes to hers. Yes, those were real eyes. And those were real shoulders there under that blue short-sleeved uniform, and a real chest. Very real. Just because she could, she ran an index finger down his arm, traced the line of his biceps down to his elbow.

Her tummy did a flip-flop.

"How did this happen?" she asked again. "You're here. With me. Here. Real. I can't believe this."

"Yes, I'm here. With you. We're together."

"How?"

His gaze dropped to their joined hands. "I went to the Wise One and asked him to send you back to Michigan. Without me."

"You . . . you did? You wanted me sent away?" She pulled her hands from his. "Why? You didn't even ask me what I wanted," she whispered. She didn't understand. Why would he do that? Hadn't he said he loved her? Why was everyone making decisions for her? Without giving her a chance to say what she wanted! This was getting old. Real fast.

"I wanted you to be safe. Watching that bastard . . . stab . . ." He visibly swallowed. "I couldn't live with the knowledge that it could happen again," he continued in a shaky voice. "It was my fault he'd found you. I brought you back when I shouldn't have. But I missed you . . . so . . . much . . . I couldn't stand being away from you any longer."

She could see he was struggling to talk. He gave her a watery smile that didn't get anywhere near his eyes. His hands fisted and flexed but he didn't lift them, didn't try to touch her again.

"I'm sorry, Goddess. I'm sorry for being so damn selfish, for not thinking of your safety first. I tried to fix it. I mean, I couldn't take away what had happened, but I could prevent it from happening again. Thankfully your injuries were superficial. After seeing you were tended to by the healer, I went to the Wise One, told him I wanted you to be safe, happy. If that meant I had to live without you, then that was the way it would be. I would deal with it. Somehow."

She could sense how difficult that would've been for him. The depth of his love, the scope of his sacrifice, it was difficult to comprehend. But it was there for her to see now, reflected in his eyes. It made his decision a whole lot easier to accept. It made something else a whole lot easier to accept as well—the urge to let it all go for the first time in her life. To let someone else take care of her, to make decisions, to be her Master. There was no way he'd ever make a decision that would hurt her. She had no doubt. This was a man she could trust. In all ways. She could trust enough to be herself, to do the one thing she'd always wanted to do but feared—she could relinquish control. In the bedroom and in her life. "You did that? For me?" she whispered. "Even though you were sad when I was gone?"

"I had to."

She'd never known anyone who was capable of such self-sacrificing love. Not even her own mother. The closest she'd ever seen was her grandmother, who'd died years ago. It was wonderful. The most profound joy swelled inside her. "I don't know what to say."

"When I went to the Wise One, I told him my decision. He took you away, told me to leave him, return in one hour. I did as he told me to. Next thing I knew, he was telling me he'd found me a job as a police officer. Then he shoved me through a strange-looking door and I found myself here, in this odd but wonderful world. It took me hours to find you, but I did."

"So you're really here to stay?"

He ran his palm down her arm then hooked a finger under her chin. "You forgive me? You're happy? Happy I'm here with you?"

"Happy? Happy! I'm ecstatic!" She threw her arms around his neck and squeezed. He hugged her back with equal enthusiasm. She tipped her head to look into his eyes. "And yes, I forgive you."

His smile was so warm and genuine, it made her insides all whooshy and soft. She nuzzled his neck. His scent, combined with the way his body felt pressed against hers, made her insides all tingly and warm. Her nipples tightened into hard little nubs. Little zaps of heat charged through her body.

"Good." He kissed her forehead, grazed her bottom lip with

his thumb. She resisted the urge to nibble it. "We will start over, from the beginning, since you don't have any memories of our courtship. I have to admit, I'm a man who enjoys the chase—"

"The beginning?" she repeated, losing the battle. She let her tongue slip out and tease the tip of his thumb with shy little swipes. "Not that I mind being the chase-ee, because that's fun, too, but the very beginning? Like, before-sex beginning?"

"Yes, the very beginning," he said around a chuckle that made her knees knock. He removed his thumb from her mouth and combed his fingers through her hair. The gentle tugging felt so good. "Before sex, before we met, before everything."

"Not that I want to butt heads with you already, but what if I don't like that idea as much as you do?" She was so not thrilled with his suggestion. For a couple reasons, but the most pressing at the moment was the slick warmth gathering between her legs. It wasn't six years, but they already shared a history of sorts, and she wasn't sure that tossing that away and starting from scratch was such a great idea. She liked what they had already. Besides, at the moment, she just wanted to be close to him, in all ways. She wanted him to hold her, to touch her, to possess her.

"Mmmm. What do you want?" he asked, gently pushing her back.

"What I want"—she pulled her upper arms out of his grip and gave him a coy grin—"is to start somewhere in the middle. Say, before 'I do' but after the *we do* . . . as in, we make love." She illustrated by tracing the line down the center of his buttoned shirt, over his belt, to the bulge front and center behind the zipper of his pants. "I . . . missed you, too. And I don't want to go back to being strangers. I want this. I want us. I want to go forward."

"I see." He sounded a little breathless. "Very well. I will allow you this small concession." He stood.

"Thank you," she said, working at his belt. "Would it be too much to ask . . ." When she had his pants unsnapped and unzipped, she was pleased to see his cock seemed to be happy to go along with her plan. "Do you think you could still call me goddess? I kinda liked it." She pushed down his pants and underwear. Black, snug, sexy.

"Sure, my goddess," he said in his deep, rumbly bear voice. He caught her wrist just before she wrapped her fingers around his erection. "On one condition." He slanted her a wicked grin that made her heart skip a few beats. "You call me Master. Now run!" Still sporting that grin, he pushed her from him. She squealed and sprinted across the living room, giggling like a goof. She got about five feet before he scooped her up into his arms and carried her into her bedroom.

"Oh!" She sucked in a surprised gasp when he laid her flat on her back on the bed and pushed a knee between her thighs.

Her girl parts sent out the welcome wagon. Her brain shut down.

Master. He wanted her to accept him as her Master. There was no man on Earth she could accept as Master but Xur. She tried to answer, tried to tell him that, but her tongue lodged itself somewhere in her throat. Nothing was getting past it. Air, sound, nada.

She guessed he interpreted her silence as acceptance, because before she knew it, they were both undressed and he was kissing her. His tongue was doing things no tongue should be able to do. Dancing in her mouth and stirring up potent lust. And in combination with lips, teeth, she could barely keep from throwing herself at him and begging for mercy.

"Do you accept me as your Master?" he repeated.

"Yes." She struggled to focus her eyes. She was light-headed and giddy, melting, trembling. A fever was building inside her and she wanted relief. Now. Not a half hour from now. Not even five minutes from now. She rocked her hips back and forth, grinding her wet pussy against his very erect cock. "To hell with the chase. I surrender. Take me," she begged between little teasing kisses and nips. When he didn't answer, she bit his shoulder.

He growled and pinched her nipple. "You have no idea how to surrender. But I will teach you."

She shuddered. Oh, the joy this man gave her! "Take me," she repeated.

"How soon you forget." He lifted his upper body off her, removed his mouth from where it had been just seconds before—her neck, where it was doing some wonderful things—and gave her a frown. "Master. I am your Master. And you must address me as such whenever we are in this room."

"Oh, yes. Master. How could I forget?"

He frowned. "To make sure you won't forget again, I am going to punish you." He lowered himself until his face was inches from hers. "This time, I'm going to bring you to the point of climax but I won't let you come," he whispered. "You may not come until I say so. You will never forget how to address me after tonight."

The sharp tone of his voice, packaged with the fire burning in his eyes and the promise in his words just about vaporized her.

"And to make sure you don't . . . take matters into your own hands at any point," he said, sitting up again. "I'm going to have to tie your wrists, like so." He caught both of her wrists and pinned them to the bed above her head. "Where are your restraints?"

"Uh. I don't have any."

"You must." It took him maybe three long strides to get to her closet. He grumbled something to himself as he sifted through her clothes. Finally, he returned with his handcuffs in one fist and the silk scarf she'd bought on a whim but never worn in the other. "These will do. For now. We will get you some more effective restraints later." He eyed the headboard, grunted in male satisfaction and then scooped her up and deposited her higher up on the mattress.

She gleefully watched his scrumptious muscles work as he secured her arms. Then she squirmed as he set about torturing her.

He started at her neck. Biting and nibbling until goose bumps covered every square inch of skin she possessed. Next, he focused his attention on her breasts. He kneaded them, pinched and pulled at her nipples, then laved at them like a cat drinking milk until her blood was like lava. It simmered in her veins, carrying heat to every part of her body.

He then kissed a path down her stomach but stopped just before reaching her pussy. "Before I go any further, perhaps we should come up with a new safe word?"

"New? What?"

"Since we are now in Michigan, I don't suppose that one's such a good idea. You have an idea for another one?"

She dragged her heavy eyelids up and gave him a surprised stare. "Are you kidding me? You expect me to think? Now? I'm at death's door. I can't think now. You come up with one."

"Very well." He visibly searched the room. His face lit up as his gaze rested on her clock. "Sony."

"Great. Sony. Got it. Can I use it now?"

"Only if you wish me to stop."

"Yes. No. No, I don't. Commence the torture, Master. Please."

Being both cruel and kind, he complied. He pushed her legs apart and gave her pussy a long swipe with his tongue. Then he parted her labia and danced his tongue over her clit.

"Oh, God," she moaned. "Oh, God, ohgod, ohgod." She

tossed her head from side to side. Climax was inevitable. The final telltale flash of heat swooped up her chest and over her face. She sucked in a breath and prepared herself for the glory that would be her orgasm.

And then he stopped.

Her pussy twitched but didn't spasm. Robbed!

"Argh!" she shouted. She lifted her head and gave her very bad husband a death stare. "Sony, Sony, Sony! That was not nice! Not. Nice. You better finish what you started, buster."

He gave her a death stare right back. "Talk to me like that, and I'll have to punish you more severely."

"Nothing could be worse than this," she whispered, making sure to say it quiet enough for him not to hear. Softened her expression, too. When he didn't say anything else, like, "Okay, you've suffered enough," she added, louder this time, "Seriously. I'm dying here. I was so close."

"Yet, you've forgotten the lesson I have tried to teach you."

"No . . ." She struggled to remember what that lesson was. It took her a few, but she finally regained the use of enough gray matter to remember. "No, I haven't forgotten. Master. I'm sorry. This is all very new. But I will try harder. I want to surrender to you. Surrender it all, my very life. You are my Master, in all ways."

He nodded his head, his expression softening. "I love you, my goddess. As your Master, I will take care of you for the rest of your days. Your needs will be mine. Your wishes. Your worries."

She blinked back a tear. She hated crying. "Thank you, for leaving your life on Celestine, for following me here." She smiled as she watched him climb onto the bed and kneel next to her legs. He looked at her with such warmth and love in his eyes. As she gazed into them, she saw the depth of his devotion. Of his commitment to her.

He genuinely loved her. Like, loved with all his heart and soul and spirit. With the kind of self-sacrificing dedication she'd never seen before from a man. She realized something else, too. She had been searching for him, long before she'd been taken back to Celestine. Longing for him. Missing him. She needed him. He was her life. He made her the woman she was meant to be.

They shared a smile.

"I am yours," she whispered. "My life, my future, my everything. It's been such a short time but I feel like I've known you forever. I . . . love you. Thank you for coming. Thank you for finding me."

"And I love you, too, my goddess." He teased her slit with the head of his cock and she arched her back, anxious for him to enter her. "You are my life," he said. "Don't you see that yet? I didn't leave my life when I left Celestine. I followed it."

"Yes. I see that now. But you still left behind the world and life you knew to come here."

He hooked his fingers under her chin and stared into her eyes. "I followed you. To this wonderful place. We will be together for the rest of our lives. We will make a life together." He unfolded his hands, revealing the delicate chain she'd worn in Celestine. "I brought something for you."

"You did. I was afraid it had been lost. If you'll untie me—"

He shook his head. "I'll do the honors."

As she trembled and quaked with pent-up desire, he suckled her right nipple until it was a hard pink point. Then he clipped the first clamp to her nipple and moved on to the left.

It was as if there was a direct connection between her pussy and nipples. The pinch of the clamp sent little bursts of heat through her body, down between her legs.

"Spread your legs," he demanded. He held the third clamp between his finger and thumb.

She knew the intense pleasure-pain that last one would bring her. Whimpering, she parted her knees and sucked in her stomach.

He bent over, and releasing the chain, gently parted her labia to expose her clit. "Do you have a vibrator? I want to tease you a bit more first."

"More teasing?" she asked weakly.

"Yes, more. You deserve it for the lack of respect you show me. Vibrator."

Since her hands were secured up over her head, there wasn't any chance she could point to anything. Jerking her head to one side was the only option she had. "Nightstand drawer," she said.

Luckily for her, he got the drift. The mattress bounced when he hopped down to the floor, reminding her of the fact that she really, really needed a new mattress set. Impatiently, he rummaged through the drawer filled with magazines and whatever else she'd stuffed in there, until he found the little pink vibrator, no doubt at the very bottom of the drawer, in the back. "Aha!" he proclaimed, holding it up like it was some friggin' major discovery or something.

The man was really too cute. And too sexy. Mrrrowwww!

Giving her this hot, "I'm going to make you suffer" look, he returned to his position on the bed, twisted the bottom of the toy and adjusted the intensity of the vibrations to maximum speed. She could tell by the pitch of the hum. Her mouth went dry as she watched him smooth some lube on the tip. He wiped the excess on his cock. A couple strokes down to the base and then up to the tip. Oy, if he expected her to last more than two seconds before coming, he was in for a surprise.

"Goddess or not, you're still expected to respect me as your Master. Since your return, you've been sarcastic and willful, you've forgotten how to address me. I realize you've suffered the loss of your memory, but I intend to teach you quickly what it means to submit." He ran the very tip of the buzzing toy around her vagina, down toward her anus then back up toward her clit. Of course, because he wanted her to suffer, no doubt, he made sure to steer clear of her clitoris.

Her inner muscles clenched and unclenched as anticipation swept through her body. The pinching of her nipples worked to intensify the frustration.

Her husband was so mean! But she sure was enjoying it.

"So tell me now, goddess. Have you learned your lesson yet?" he murmured in that low, husky voice of his. He made another circle around her pussy with the vibrator, this time letting the tip skim across her clit. White-hot sparks of need scattered through her body. "Or do I need to punish you some more?"

"Ye-yes, Master." Her eyelids were too heavy to hold up. She let them fall closed. Her stomach tightened. She tipped her hips up, spread her legs wider.

"More punishment? Very well."

"No! No, Master. I meant no, you don't need to punish me anymore."

"I believe I do. I believe you want me to." This time he let the vibrator remain on her clit for several seconds, long enough to make her shake. Then he pushed the toy inside her pussy and applied the clamp to her clit.

She pressed her feet to the mattress and bucked, pushing her pelvis high into the air. The little sparks were now giant infernos and they didn't scatter like hot metal shards, they swept through her like explosions. "Eey! Ohhhh!" she screeched. The chains caught with her motion and tugged on both nipples and clit, creating even more intensity.

She was going to die! Her heart was going to race out of control, her lungs were going to collapse, and she was going to expire. Right there. "Oh, please, Master. Please!"

"Please what, goddess? Please more? Very well."

"No . . ." She opened her eyes.

He settled himself between her legs, squirted some lube onto her anus and then pushed a finger slowly into her hole.

Her anus burned a tiny bit as it stretched, but the pain was just one more sensation added to the already overwhelming flurry that she was swimming in. The sharp pinching at her nipples, clit. The sound of his groans as he stroked his cock. The vibrations deep inside her vagina. The sight of his tight expression as he looked down at her pussy.

He pulled his finger out. "Goddess, I can't wait another minute. I must fuck you. Now. In your ass."

She put up a silent prayer of thanks.

He entered her with a slow, deliriously decadent thrust. His cock filled her completely, stirring up the embers of the fire that he had allowed to die down. The rising heat spread out, out from her center, up her stomach, over her chest.

With each slow inward thrust, he drove her body closer, closer to release. And when she trembled on the verge of climax, he murmured in her ear, "That's it, love. Turn yourself over to me. Let yourself go. Come for me."

She sighed, overcome by the pleasure of her climax, and clung to him, wrapping her legs around his waist to welcome his cock deeper inside. Her pussy spasmed around the vibrator, and she felt his cock swell slightly as he found his release. It was glorious. It was beyond words.

When all the toys and paraphernalia had been removed, and she was lying a sated, tingling blob of delighted goo, she kissed his face, just as he had done after the first time they'd made love. His eyes. His nose. His chin and forehead. "My refuge. My protector. My friend. My Master."

"My naughty goddess." He stretched and groaned, like a large, sated man was prone to do. "Tonight, you will not surrender so easily. I want a real chase."

She squirmed, heating again at the thought of him chasing her around the house—correction, it was the thought of him catching her *after* chasing her through the house that had her squirming. "Fair enough."

"Good." He gave her a satisfied nod. "Then there's only one other matter to discuss."

"Oh?"

"That of our second wedding. I wish to set the date, so that we are able to make preparations. Since your memory of our first ceremony has been erased, I want this one to be special, a day you could never forget. What is the tradition here? In this world? In Celestine it is the groom's responsibility to plan the wedding. It is a very private event, attended by only the couple's very closest friends and family."

"The tradition here is the exact opposite. We get married in a church in front of hundreds of people. And the bride takes a good year or two to plan the wheres, whos and whens of it all, with the help of her maid of honor and mother. But this is what I'm thinking," she said, snuggling closer to his warmth. "I don't want a traditional wedding as much as I always thought I did. How about we forget about planning, and I'll take a week or two off work, and you surprise me? I have all the faith in the world that I'll love what you plan, just like I did before."

"As you wish, my goddess. As you wish."

"And then, afterward, I think I might need a little more of your very special brand of punishment. You know, because I'll probably need a reminder about respecting my Master. I hate to say it, but I think it could take a few weeks, months even, before I get it right." A grin pulling at her mouth, she jumped up from the bed and dashed for the door. "But you'll have to catch me first!"

His laughter rumbled down the hall after her. "How I love a good chase. Run, my naughty goddess. You will be punished," he said almost directly behind her, "when I catch you."

TEMPTING A LADY

DAWN RYDER

ONE

"MY SWEET, SAY YES."

"I shouldn't." A giggle betrayed how little Annabelle meant her words. Standing in the shadows, Emma frowned at the predator holding her sister. Oh yes, Lord Shackhorn was a creature who set traps and then feasted on his catch. Disguised by a century-old fine name, the man was, in truth, no gentleman.

"Now, Annabelle, a goddess such as you is above rules. I want to worship you. Let me be your devoted servant." Herbert Shackhorn clasped Annabelle's head between his hands and covered her mouth with his. It was no simple kiss but a blunt invasion of the younger girl's carefully guarded innocence. Emma glared around the garden looking for the maid who should have been trailing her sister by her order, but the good-for-nothing servant was nowhere to be seen. It was little wonder. Along with that fine name went a rather heavy fortune that Herbert was well-known for sharing with those who allowed him to debauch at his whim. The man even had a title. Americans should have been above needing such a thing but society was quite willing to bend over for the English lord's pleasure, granting him forgiveness in the face of the rumors that clung to his coattails.

Yet not at her father's home would Herbert find his title opening the thighs of the younger daughter while silencing the cries of her family. Annabelle was young and silly but she was also chaste and Emma intended it to remain exactly that way. Emma lifted a single hand and pushed a clay-potted fern off its spot atop a ledge. It slammed into the cobblestones with a crash that startled Herbert into breaking off his hungry kiss. His eyes reminded her of a jackal as he glared at her, and Emma studied the look to remind herself of what men truly were. Carnivores set on a meal. They hid it behind their gentlemanly ways, but after the wedding came the unveiling as the sheets were pulled back, and even the church blessed their animalistic gorging.

"Emma . . . I'm so sorry . . . yet I was looking for Tellie. She wandered away and I feared for her," Annabelle stammered with nervous fear as she looked to Herbert for assistance. The English lord left her to flounder on her own.

Emma smiled sweetly at her sister as she reached for the crooked neckline of her evening dress. Steady fingers smoothed the India silk into order as Emma pulled the fabric up to conceal Annabelle's nipples. The current fashion only made it simpler for men to steal a younger girl's attention with a swift plunge into her bodice. The empire waistline cupped the breasts, lifting them into prominent display that Emma found rather unsuitable for a girl of fifteen like Annabelle, yet society found no fault in it.

"I will see to Tellie. Father was just looking for you, so hurry along and find him before he worries and sends his men searching for you."

The frozen look of terror on Annabelle's face melted away as she smiled at her sister. "Oh, Emma, you are the best sister ever!" She flung her arms around her and squeezed Emma's neck before there was a flutter of blue silk as Annabelle ran toward the ballroom and the music spilling out of the open patio doors. Emma stared at Herbert Shackhorn until her sister's steps faded into the noise of her father's guests. She dropped him a smooth curtsy before turning her back on the man. Ooh, her temper strained against her good judgment, yet Emma picked up each foot and forced her body away from him. With a few words, the lord might blacken her sister's name beyond repair. Society always sided with money. Her father was not poor but his name was nowhere as near as blue as Herbert Shackhorn's, so she would say nothing to him and find contentment in knowing she had ruined his plans to seduce her sister.

At least for the moment. An entire week stretched out in front of her like the vast Sahara Desert with endless opportunities for the man to tumble Annabelle. The brandy would flow and the gentlemen would charm their way into more than just hearts.

And then they would try to flee from the marriage noose. Loading into their carriages and riding off to the next host in a summer-long party that was the fashion in 1808. Poetry and dancing, wafer-thin dresses, but the most surprising thing was that love was now in fashion. It was embraced as men such as Lord Byron became a celebrated source of inspiration. That tender emotion had always been forbidden by a society held together by profitable marriages, but society had suddenly found tolerance for young lovers.

Well, not completely. Emma smiled on her way back to her father's party. The stable master's daughter still did not wed the lord's son but a lady with a good name might indeed catch herself a fine lord if Cupid were of a mind to help matters along. It was a dream that danced through young girls' heads, but one of which Emma knew the harsher side.

Emma smiled as she drew close enough to hear the music

clearly. Life really was full of little delights that made up for the disappointments that she'd encountered in her short marriage. Truly, she should have expected that reality wouldn't live up to her dreams—nothing in life ever did.

Moving onto the patio, Emma watched the couples floating by as they danced. The girls' eyes shimmered as they dreamed of husbands who devoted themselves to endless summers of love.

But the men . . . Oh, Emma knew what they fantasized about. Nature had gifted the human male with a dark side that craved a more primitive manner of contact between the genders. When the doors were closed and their prey was in hand, those very same gentlemen would rut like beasts, holding their female in place as they fucked like hounds.

Emma could not change nature but she could direct Lord Herbert Shackhorn's attention away from Annabelle. Being a widow offered Emma so much freedom and she intended to indulge herself in it. Yes, her dearly deceased husband's mother had sent her packing but Emma was delighted to be home. Her father needed her to run his estate now that her own mother was gone. It was a role Emma thrived in. Oh, it was not the grandest house her father owned—those he had left to her two brothers—but this was a home and Emma praised her luck that her sire was as happy with the arrangement as she was. There was no further urging for her to marry. She had done so and fate had decided to break those chains.

It didn't matter to Emma. Great position had never held any mesmerizing appeal to her. Her widow's inheritance, intelligently invested, would support her through the years. Yet best of all was the fashion of love. Emma might hide behind it forever and refuse to marry again as long as society believed she harbored a deep and burning affection for her departed husband.

A giggle rose from her throat as Emma stepped into the ballroom. It was amazing the things you could make people believe without ever opening your lips. All she had to do was say nothing at all and the gossips would do the rest. The old ladies would mutter about her love for a man long dead, sympathizing over her lingering in widowhood because she could not bear to marry any other.

Ha! The only thing that held her away from another marriage was the fact that she would once again have to submit to the harsh touch of a man. Emma pitied the whores who had to endure in order to eat. Well, she was not hungry and her body would never be used by a man's lust again.

And Lord Shackhorn would not be using Annabelle, either. Not while Emma could do anything about it.

IT WASN'T HARD TO FOLLOW Herbert away from the party. The man was full of his own pride and made plenty of noise as he stomped up the grand staircase. Emma twitched up her skirt and took the back stairs in quick steps and she still beat the man to the second story, where his room was. She ran on silent feet toward her own room as she went to put on her dressing gown. Her dress was tailored for practicality as well as fashion and Emma slipped it off before discarding her few undergarments. The cool night air made her shiver as she shrugged into her dressing gown and gave the belt a swift tie. Her mother's ghost was going to rise and haunt her but Emma didn't care. Lord Herbert was going to be brought to her heel and there was only one way she could think to force the man to her will.

Opening the servant door at the back of her room, Emma stood in the hallway and waited for her eyes to adjust. Luck was with her because a candle flickered in one of the overhead holders from the staff moving back and forth to service the ladies retiring from the ball. Checking for any witnesses, Emma scurried toward the back entrance to the suite Lord Herbert was in. His father was a great name in Virginia and Emma had made certain the man would not find fault with his accommodations while under her father's roof. So, Herbert was sleeping right next to the family rooms and that fit her designs . . . perfectly.

There was a small manservant chamber attached to the suite, just enough room for a cot and dressing closet. Such attached chambers were rather common on grander estates where all members of the family could afford to have a servant who saw to their personal needs and was expected to be at hand at all times. A curtain hung over the slim doorway and Emma could see the flicker of candlelight through its coarse weave. Her stocking-clad feet made no sound as she crept closer to that curtain to peer in at her prey.

"Get on your knees, Tellie, my cock is swollen enough to kill me."

The maid Emma had been searching for gave a husky laugh before she obeyed Herbert and knelt before him. He smirked at the top of her head as the maid began to unfasten his night drawers. Her nimble fingers made swift work of the buttons holding the garment closed over his crotch, and a moment later she reached into the opening to pull Herbert's cock into view. Emma angled her head so that she might view the odd performance with both eyes through the edge of the curtain and the doorjamb.

"Your Lordship didn't enjoy the garden as much as you planned?" Tellie was being extremely bold, but considering she was fingering Herbert's cock, Emma wasn't sure just what to think. The maid moved her fingers all the way down the length of the staff and then cupped the twin sacs hanging beneath the rod before she closed her grip around the staff once again and pulled her hand up Herbert's cock to the crown.

Herbert gasped and rubbed Tellie's head like a favored pet. The girl smiled rather smugly as she looked at the cock in her grip. "Your damn mistress has the worst timing." Herbert gasped as Tellie worked her hand down his cock and back up.

"Suck it already, woman!" Herbert hissed his command but Emma caught that smug smile brightening Tellie's face once again. Herbert couldn't see the sly expression and Tellie opened her mouth and licked the top of Herbert's cock with the tip of her tongue. The man growled like a mongrel dog getting a good patting from its master.

"That's it, suck my cock."

Tellie licked the head instead. Her tongue made a slow circle around the ridge that made up the crown before she flickered her tongue right up the center slit. She worked her hands up and down the staff as she licked and Emma got the idea that the maid was deliberately lingering over her licks because she was, in fact, the one in control. Herbert shuddered as his hips thrust his cock into the kneeling maid's face, but Tellie only licked the head of his cock once again.

"Christ, Tellie! Double your price! Just suck my cock, you bitch!"

That smile appeared once more and then Tellie opened her mouth and took the head of Herbert's cock between her lips. Her hand clamped around the staff and prevented Herbert from thrusting his entire cock into her open mouth. Instead the maid remained in control as she worked her lips around the head and crown of the cock. Herbert growled but his hand fisted in the maid's hair as she worked her hands on the portion that wasn't inside her mouth.

"Good . . . good . . . use your tongue."

Tellie opened her mouth and took more of the cock inside. She actually moved her head back and forth, taking more length and pulling her closed mouth along it until she was at the tip, before plunging back down the staff. Herbert gripped her head as he thrust his hips in time with her, fucking her mouth.

Emma was held to the display out of sheer curiosity. Tellie looked as though she was completely in control and that fascinated her. Emma had always pitied a whore her plight, but Tellie was likely earning a fair bit for tonight's duty and the girl looked as if she knew exactly how to handle Herbert.

"Enough! I'll not spill in your mouth tonight, Tellie! It's your pussy that is going to be earning that double price. Get up and hike your skirt." Herbert used his grip on the maid's hair to pull her away from his cock. The head came free of her mouth with a little pop as Herbert kept pulling on her hair. A frown covered Tellie's face before she stood up. A small smack broke the silence in the room as Herbert lightly struck her on one side of her face. He snickered at her gasp and pointed at the large bed behind her.

"Thought you could suck me off, didn't you?" Herbert snickered again as he pushed his drawers down his legs and stepped out of them. He left them pooled on the floor as he ripped his shirt over his head and threw it aside. The man gave no care for the force he used and Emma heard a small tearing of the fine fabric.

"Well, not Herbert Shackhorn! I'm not a drunken sailor fresh into port who you can earn that much silver from with a quick tongue. Get on your back and show me what I've bought tonight. I want to see the pussy that is going to take my cock and you'd better not stink of the pox."

"I'm clean."

Herbert smacked Tellie once again. "Get on your back and hike your skirts. I'll see for myself before I fuck you. You'd better not have the curse, either."

Tellie didn't say anything else, but gathered up her skirt in her hands before climbing onto the raised surface of the bed. She left her legs hanging over the side of the thick mattress with her bottom on the edge as she pulled her skirt above her waist and spread her thighs.

"That's much better. I like to see what I buy." Herbert moved a candle closer to the spread woman and Emma couldn't stop her eyes from following. She had no idea what her body looked like when the thighs were wide apart like that. Tellie's body glistened in the candlelight and there were two fat folds of flesh that shielded the opening to her womb. Herbert slid a finger right up the center of those folds and then thrust it into the channel where men like to plunge their cocks. Emma remembered it well from her years as a wife; her husband would press her down into the mattress as he spread her thighs and then fit the head of his cock against that opening before using his hips and back to drive the thick pole deep into her body. Herbert pulled his fingers free and brought them up to his nose to sniff.

"Well, you smell clean and no blood of your monthly curse, either." Herbert snickered as he sat the candle back on its table. He stroked his hand up the inside of one of Tellie's thighs as he smirked at the spread display before him.

"Let's fuck." Herbert fit his cock against Tellie's body and shoved it deep. Emma felt her body jerk as she remembered the pain that came with the first few thrusts. Tellie's knees bounced and she muttered softly as Emma caught the slap of wet flesh against wet flesh.

"Damn juicy pussy." Herbert fucked the maid hard as she

gasped and actually raised her bottom for his thrusts. He leaned over her body, bracing his hands on either side of her torso as his buttocks tightened and contracted with his fucking.

"Work your ass, bitch! If I want to fuck a log, I'll get married! Thrust that pussy up here!"

Tellie worked her bottom fast and further up off the bed. The bed curtains swung with their motions as Herbert grunted and snarled with his fucking. For endless moments they sounded like beasts, and the bed ropes creaked as Herbert drove his cock in and out of Tellie's body. The maid worked her bottom in time as her fingers clawed at the comforter beneath her. There was a final snarl from Herbert as he shoved his cock deep into Tellie and his entire body shuddered.

Herbert gasped for several moments before he pulled free and stomped across the room. He yanked something from his coat that was neatly hung and then moved back to where Tellie was sitting up and moving off the bed. He flung something at her and Emma heard the metallic sound of coins hitting the floor. The maid frantically chased the coins, grasping at the money with no care for her modesty.

"Now get out."

Tellie didn't waste any time doing what Herbert told her to do. The maid straightened her linen cap before tucking her money into her bodice. Her skirt fell back into place and, that quickly, she looked prim and proper. No one might have guessed that she'd just been a-fucking.

Herbert moved toward a crystal decanter sitting nearby. A small candle kept the wine warm and he poured himself a large glass of it. Emma suppressed a giggle at the little touch that she had ordered be placed in the suite. She certainly hadn't suspected that Tellie would use the chore of delivering the wine as a chance to earn money on her back. It was such a wicked little bit of knowledge and Emma found it funny as well. Weren't humans such odd creatures? They were like actors on the stage, presenting one image while they were intent on doing quite the opposite.

Emma frowned as she looked at Herbert. The hard facts of his ungentlemanly intentions were not amusing when it came to Annabelle. Herbert hid his debauchery behind his father's good name. Emma reached for the curtain as she grasped at her courage and stepped into the room. A man like Herbert needed to be handled like the base creature he was.

"How very interesting, I did wonder where Tellie ran off to tonight when she was set to looking after Annabelle. It is a good thing your father is so free with his money." Emma walked right up to the bed and clicked her tongue as she looked at the mussed bedding.

"Good God, woman! What would your father say?" Herbert's eyes were bulging from his head and Emma smiled at his shock.

"I imagine my father would be most unhappy to find me here . . . especially with the room smelling of your lust. Men seem to have ways of knowing just what the scent smells like. Father always knows when fucking has been going on in a room."

"I didn't lay a hand on you!"

Emma bit into her lip as she undid the knot in her belt. There was only one way to ensure Herbert would leave her sister in peace and the price was going to be her modesty. She untied the belt and let her robe flutter to her feet. Herbert hissed as her nude body glimmered in the candlelight.

"But you have been fucking. Is there any way to prove exactly whom? Do you think anyone would believe you, Herbert, if I pointed my finger at you?"

"Of course they would!"

Emma laughed as she ran a finger over the soiled bed. "I doubt that. However, do feel at ease to test your theories. Cry out and see if my father doesn't insist you marry me."

"You bitch! Well, you won't get a title from me. Maybe I should toss you on your back and teach you what happens to ladies who act like strumpets."

Emma lowered her eyes to Herbert's cock. The organ lay soft and quite spent between his legs. She raised an eyebrow at his temper. "With what? Not that flaccid cock. However, I have no desire to be shackled to you for the rest of my life. No, Herbert, I am here to make quite certain you understand that my sister will be a virgin when you depart at the end of the week. As you can see, I am very dedicated to this cause. If I must place my own body between you and her, I shall. You will not soil her."

"Or you will do what, perchance?" Herbert snickered as he ran his eyes down the length of her nude body. The gesture was meant to humiliate her but Emma held to her strength. She did not crave this creature's approval—only his compliance.

"Do you know who runs this house?" Emma tossed her head and propped a hand on her hip. "I do. There is nothing I am afraid to do, my fine blue-blooded lord. Standing here naked isn't too high a price when it comes to my sister. Be assured if you trifle with Annabelle even once more, I will be back in this very spot and I will scream the house down! Even your father's money won't save you from the scandal."

"Nor you!"

Emma grinned before she bent and picked up her robe. She slipped her arms into it and covered her body now that her point had been made. When dealing with a sniveling mongrel like Herbert, you needed to get his attention before he would be brought to heel. "I do not care, sir. Gladly would I suffer the scandal as long as it keeps my sister from becoming your latest toy."

"I didn't hurt the girl." Herbert sniffed and tossed the remaining wine in his goblet into his mouth. There was a slight tremble in his arm as he reached for the decanter to refill the glass.

"I am glad we understand each other. Remember that Annabelle is a child and I will remember to make certain Tellie is assigned to this wing of the house during your stay."

Herbert's eyes brightened as he frowned. "You're quite a bitch." His words were laced with male pride as he glared at her.

"I would do anything for my family, sir. That was the point of my visit tonight. Call me bitch, yet I do not let my actions shame my parents like the rumors say yours do. Leave my sister in her chaste innocence or I do assure you, I will be back and the next maid who enters this chamber will be old enough to be your grandmother."

Emma walked from the room as she listened to Herbert curse her. She refused to care. The man wasn't worth a single moment of concern. True, her actions were low but when dealing with a gutter scoundrel, it was necessary to fling mud right along with them.

Annabelle was worth it.

"YOU ARE A DISGRACE, Herbert."

Herbert Shackhorn snapped to attention as his brother's words sliced through the dark room. It was his worst nightmare that materialized from the shadows in the form of his elder brother Julian Stanley, the Baron Strange. A man too large and bulky for the current fashion of graceful gentlemen, Julian was a huge menace who glared at him with the disapproval of the one person about whose opinion Herbert cared—his father, the Earl of Derby.

"Did you have to try and seduce your host's youngest daughter?" Julian moved closer like a lion circling a wounded water buffalo. "It would appear that Father was correct about one thing—you do need to be taken in hand." Julian's lips lifted into a rare grin. "But I'm rather pleased to have witnessed the fact that there is at least one American who found the backbone to spit in your eye, brother mine."

"Piss off, Julian. That bitch needs to be taken down a peg or two and I've a mind to see the task done personally." Herbert lifted his chin in the face of his brother's displeasure. The gleam in Julian's eyes made his stomach twist though, because Herbert knew all too well that Julian wasn't a man who took insults lightly. More than one man had discovered that trait in his elder brother as Julian's fist connected with his face. Herbert sniffed in arrogant pride—Julian was his half brother, the product of a lesser marriage to a girl somewhat lacking in true blue English blood. Their shared father had professed love for the girl and run off the Scottish border to wed her before the family could make him see reason. Herbert sniffed again as he looked at the wide shoulders that Julian had inherited from his mother's blood. It was the sort of frame better suited to a man forced to earn his way in the world with labor, so very unrefined, unlike his own slim build.

"You will treat that lady with the very deepest respect, Herbert." Julian's voice had dipped into an icy tone that made Herbert's heart accelerate in response. Common blood or not, Julian was ruthless in business, and the money their father lavished on Herbert came from his brother's brutal nature that shunned society in favor of building the family empire. Herbert needed that money and this was the tone that Julian used when he was in the mood to cut him off if Herbert didn't comply with his wishes. Herbert made certain to avoid Julian's path just so he didn't have to worry about his brother's goodwill. He far preferred not thinking about Julian at all. Most of the time Julian shared that opinion, but it appeared the gossips had done their job well enough to ruffle his father's feathers and have Julian dispatched. His older brother was also the old lord's strong-arm man when it came to snapping the family into obedience. The lord knew Julian was built for it—too tall, his shoulders too wide and there was the thick muscle covering his body. Even the best-tailored coat couldn't hide the bulges of strength Julian gained from taking his hands-on approach to stallions and shipping. It was so . . . common.

"She's not worth a quarrel between family, Julian."

"Yes, she is." Julian stepped up close enough to see the fear flickering in his younger sibling's eyes. Disgust bloomed in him for the weakness he could smell on Herbert's skin. He was pathetic, wallowing in his pride and completely blind to the brilliance of the female who had just faced him down. The fire blazing from her eyes was still branded on Julian's brain as he considered the sheer joy it would be to ride her. She was the sort of woman who would never let a weak-kneed fop like Herbert between her thighs. Julian felt his cock thicken in response. He had no use for the whining gold diggers who flocked to the well-tailored gentlemen like Herbert. Their blood was weakened by their greed, but not the creature who had just brazened her path in front of his brother's nose. Now that was a woman worth hunting.

"Not one finger, Herbert, nor a single cross word will you lay upon her name. Is that very clear, brother?"

"You're mad, do you know that, Julian? That bitch shucked her clothing like a dockside hussy. How can you possibly be interested in her? Or is it just a hard cock driving you? Hmmm? The desire to fuck her into submission—well, that is understandable. I'd like to rut her for the humiliation effect myself."

Herbert never saw the blow coming. Julian's fist connected with his chin in a mind-numbing impact that sent Herbert onto the polished wooden floorboards. Herbert cussed as his mouth filled with blood and his lips twisted with anger. He would be forced to leave before anyone saw his face. A gentleman of the season did not ever have bruises on his face. That was so . . . common. "Bastard."

"No, I'm quite legitimate much to your lady mother's displeasure. Now get out and remember, Herbert, I will track you down if you lay any rumors upon that lady's name." Julian moved back toward the shadows he'd melted from. His boots didn't even make a sound. Herbert got to his feet.

"She's more in common with a dock hussy than any gently bred lady! You saw it yourself!"

Julian turned so that only half his face was illuminated by the candlelight. It made him even more sinister and Herbert took a step away from the intensity burning in his eyes. "Very true, Herbert, she isn't a lady . . . yet. But I intend to remedy that."

"You're mad!"

Julian grinned. Maybe he was but he was going to pursue the source of his current insanity and discover just why she intoxicated him so completely. His cock throbbed with the need to discover what the ride was like between the vixen's thighs. It would put every other female he'd ever fucked to shame, Julian knew that deep in his gut. The image of her nude body danced in his memory as he enjoyed the burn of arousal it unleashed. She was magnificent, bold and fearless like a Valkyrie from legend. The sort of blood that called to his and demanded the most primal of responses.

To give chase. Julian growled softly as he heard his brother cussing. Yes, she was far too fine a treasure to leave to males who did not value her strength. Julian understood the blood racing through her body and the loyalty that had sent her into Herbert's room. Even her modesty was discarded in the face of her family's name. That was true honor, the kind he craved to have mixed with his own blood. No quarter asked or yielded. Julian grinned as his cock jerked.

She was his perfect mate.

TWO

HOLDING HER FACE CALM was an art for which Emma felt certain she lacked true talent. Oh, she practiced in front of her dressing mirror every morning, and yet at times when her mind was completely bored, she felt her composure slipping as her true feelings attempted to emerge onto her face.

This afternoon was a perfect example of a test of her resolve to maintain her public image. Emma struggled against the need to squirm in her seat as the gentlemen continued to read their poetry. Dearest saints above! Emma had reached her limit half an hour past. While she could admire the wit it took to write the rhyming couplets, she simply did not have any true liking for it. Oh, but it was all the rage among the fashionable! Poetry to inspire the heart to love! Tender words designed to romance a delicate lady because the flesh was crude but the heart pristine. Emma let her eyes move over the guests in the room, and she stared at the ladies' dewy eyes in complete astonishment. They cast adoring looks at the men reading their latest works of poetry, as Emma sat wishing a maid would appear in the doorway to summon her away from the torment of listening to any more rhyming couplets.

Perhaps she did not have a tender heart. It would explain so many things. Emma held back a tiny sigh. She simply did not understand herself at times. During an era when love was allowed, she found herself quite content to live without it. Emma simply did not understand what it was about the fumbling touches of a man that caused other women to look so lovingly at them. There were other married women who, in fact, looked as if they did love their husbands, but all Emma could recall was the rather blunt contact her late husband had pressed onto her once they were alone in their bed. Sex was nothing she longed for.

Someone stepped into the doorway and Emma was already rising from her seat before she realized it was not a member of the household staff. He wore a wool coat and stood far enough back that no one in the room could see his features clearly. A few of the ladies offered her sympathetic nods before they returned to their adoring admiration of the current gentleman reader. Emma offered a small curtsy to the gentlemen before she walked quietly from the room, attempting to contain her relief. Whoever was in the doorway, he was her immediate friend for his timely arrival. The blood in her legs felt as if it had turned to jelly and she was practically desperate to escape the afternoon pastime. The young gentlemen could be wooing for hours yet to come.

Her rescuer had moved out of the doorway by the time Emma got close enough to view his face. A tiny twist of disappointment crossed her thoughts because she would have liked to know who it was. He had looked right at her, she was certain of it. Perhaps that was vain of her, to think he held any interest in her, but the feeling persisted as she moved down the hallway and away from the poetry reading. Escape was at hand and Emma had no intention of losing her opportunity. The afternoon was warm and sunny, and being caged inside tormented her unfashionable desire to walk and feel those hot rays of sunlight against her cheeks. What did she care if it spoilt her creamy complexion? All of the rules for beauty felt like ropes binding her spirit and holding it captive. Casting a look down either side of the hallway, Emma let a secret smile break the calm expression on her face. She lifted her knees and scampered down the length of the hallway and outside to indulge herself in a moment of freedom from the duties as hostess.

"You are quite welcome, Emma."

The deep voice froze her. Only her eyes moved as Emma found the man from the doorway. He was standing next to the doorway that led outside but with his back to the outer wall of the house so that you could not see him from inside. A shiver shook her as Emma moved away from his large body. One corner of his mouth lifted into a half grin as he took a step away from the wall.

"Forgive me, sir, I believe we have not been introduced."

Julian held his amusement in check. He had been watching her for most of the day, only adding fuel to his quest to corner her. It was odd the way desire worked. There was the need that hardened a man's cock at night that was nothing more than a desire to fuck. Any female would do, it was an instinct to procreate and little else. His current arousal was for the creature in front of him. His cock slowly hardened as he got close enough to see her brown eyes. She nibbled on her lower lip as her eyes considered his larger size. Julian enjoyed the bit of arousal that traveled through his blood in response to the flicker of excitement that touched her face. Emma was unaware of that emotion but he wasn't, and his cock twitched with the need to get inside her. It was blunt and primitive but it was also the most intense craving he'd ever felt. He didn't just want to fuck Emma, he wanted to mate her. It was not something he deliberated over; the burning need was being carried through his bloodstream to every part of his body. The intensity rose as he moved closer to her and she shied back as a mare did from a stallion when she wasn't fully in heat for his mounting yet.

"Will you walk with me? You looked as though the poetry was about to strangle you with boredom."

His voice was polished and finished with a strong English accent with the pronunciation of a gentleman of high station. His coat was the finest wool and tailored to his large shoulders with pure perfection. But the shoulders that lurked beneath that coat were so much more than the gentlemen Emma was accustomed to finding in attendance at one of the summer parties. There was the sort of strength that she might find packed on a sailor's back from his battle against the sea and her merciless fury. Emma shook herself as she looked into the man's eyes. They were a stunning shade of topaz that looked almost like a flame flickering back at her. He held one large hand up with his offer and a tingle raced over her skin as Emma considered laying her hand in his. The flicker of that flame behind those topaz eyes said he would consider it much more than a mere afternoon stroll.

She really was insane to think such a thing of a stranger but there was something in his eyes that looked . . . untamed. A sort of challenge that he was sending toward her, and her body seemed to understand even if her brain told her she was making far too much of a simple invitation to walk. But he was a man who possessed a keen intuition—she had been bored unto tears. Emma doubted there was another soul who would have noticed it. A shiver shook her spine as she recognized that this man understood her too well. It placed a powerful weapon into his hands because he saw straight through her façade. She felt more naked in his sights just now than she had felt last night facing Herbert down.

"Julian Stanley." Although he bowed, it was not a meek offering of his name. He spoke with hardened authority, a bit as if he was giving her a lesson that he expected her to remember. His eyes flickered with some manner of exception that sent a shiver down her spine once again. Emma was amazed to feel the response because she had never once been so acutely aware of any man before. She could actually feel her cheeks warming with a blush. The hardest part of being a hostess to a summer party was the fact that guests might arrive at any time. Emma met with her head housekeeper at every chance to discover who had arrived recently, because invitations were sent not just to her father's friends but to every person of any importance. Not to be invited was the height of rudeness.

Julian missed none of those little details, either. His eyes watched her with the same keen attention of a hunting hawk, one corner of his mouth lifting as he offered his hand to her.

"Of course, if you would rather rejoin the others, I will be happy to escort you."

Emma felt her temper flicker to life because Julian was challenging her. Oh, she could not accuse him of it but she knew it! His topaz eyes were alight with knowledge of the trap he had her neatly pinned in. She was cornered by his invitation and, with no pressing need for her at hand, it would be most rude of her to decline his invitation to walk without returning to her father's other guests. The hostess did not refuse to join the party.

Emma did not take his hand. Julian grinned at her back as she clasped her gloved hands tightly in front of her and strolled past him on her way down the steps. The tight little pout on her lips was another reason his cock remained hard. Spirit. It was such an undervalued quality in ladies. He was pressing her and Emma was not going to allow him to overrun her defenses so quickly. Admiration flared to life as he used his longer strides to catch up with her.

Emma was torn. On one hand she was delighted to be free of the house. Her favorite season was spring because there were no social engagements to attend. She might walk every day and never care about her complexion.

But her company shredded the joy she normally felt as she walked. It wasn't that Julian made her angry, it was more a case that she did not feel comfortable with her eyes away from the man. It was a sort of respect for the fact that he wasn't as tame as his finely tailored coat implied he should be. Any one of the gentlemen sitting in the parlor reading poetry she would have been at ease with, but Emma almost laughed as she considered Julian sitting among them. Her eyes strayed to him as he walked beside her. Her head did not reach his shoulder and she was not a petite woman. Annabelle was but Emma favored her father too much for the current fashion. Well, that and Emma refused to wear her shoes too small, to suffer the pain in order to look dainty.

"I enjoy spirit, Emma."

Emma was startled by the comment. She turned her head completely to look at her companion. She gasped as she saw the determination on his face. Gone was any hint of playfulness. In its place was hunger. That shiver moved down her spine but this time it traveled into her passage. Emma felt empty for the first time that she could remember, and her eyes moved over Julian's mouth as she considered what his kiss must be like. It would be hard and demanding. She knew it as she stared at the wide shoulders and the strength that would allow Julian to capture her and hold her tightly against his body.

"Stop biting your lip."

"Indeed, sir."

"Julian." He barked his name like a command and hooked one hand into her elbow. With a simple step, Julian turned her, and her own momentum helped him to do it. Emma had taken three steps off the main path before she stopped herself, because she had allowed her emotions to quicken her pace. She ended between two of the large trees that lined the main drive leading to the front of her father's home. Her stomach gave a twist as Emma recognized that she was simply alone with Julian, and a quick glance at his face told her Julian was extremely pleased with his maneuver.

"There is no reason to bite your lip when with me, Emma. I enjoy your spirit so let it loose." His eyes flashed with anticipation as he looked at her mouth with that hungry glance once again. Emma gasped as she recognized that she had not been the only one thinking about a kiss. Excitement raced through her and settled in her belly. There was a tiny flicker of heat at the top of her sex that confused her. Julian was a stranger, she was mad to even think about his kiss. But, then, she was foolish to find herself so alone with him as well. It was little wonder the man looked as if he was going to steal a kiss from her; she was behaving like a common strumpet. Ladies did not walk out with strangers.

"I fear I have given you a false impression of my character. Forgive me, but I must return to the house immediately." Disappointment flashed through her but Emma scolded herself. She might have tossed convention aside last night out of desperation, but this was different. She would not follow her odd impulses into ruin.

Julian grinned at her. His eyes lit with the expression and it sent another jolt of excitement through her. This time Emma actually felt her nipples tingle before they drew into little hard buttons as though it were cold. But her skin wasn't chilled, quite the reverse, her dress felt too tight and the fabric too thick. She was almost desperate to be free of it so that she might cool off. That heat was even invading her passage, making her shift her feet farther apart because the folds of flesh that covered the opening to her body felt swollen.

"Will you marry me, Emma?"

She gasped and Julian caught her body with one arm. He wanted to shatter her composure and gain a look at the woman he'd viewed last night. Patience wasn't one of his virtues, and his desire for Emma was certainly no exception to that truth. He craved that woman like water. This calm lady wasn't to his liking, instead it was like a challenge to find the way to disrupt her control enough to touch that flame that burned inside her.

Emma ran into his chest and gasped again as her hands spread out over the thick muscle. It was too much temptation not to linger over his body for at least a tiny stolen moment. Her nose caught the warm scent of his skin and that flicker of heat at the front of her sex turned into a throb. Julian cupped her chin and raised it until their eyes met.

"Does a proposal earn me more of your company?"

"You toy with me, sir." Emma felt her face turn scarlet as she listened to her own voice. It wasn't tight with anger but husky with excitement. Her body shivered against his as her belly told her without doubt that his cock was hard. That throbbing at the front of her sex increased as she tried to curl her bottom away from his thighs. Julian shifted and placed one of his hands over her bottom to hold her body against his. She should have screamed but the only sound that emerged from her quivering body was a moan. There was so much sensation that Emma was lost as she tried to escape it, but it pulled her into its current, refusing to release her body, and her mind was drowning in it.

"I assure you, Emma, I do not play games. If marriage would gain me your company, I will face the altar with you." Julian's eyes flashed with a hard warning as his fingers tightened on her chin. "What I will not do is watch you tuck your tail between your legs and run away from me."

"What manner of man are you, sir? Certainly no gentleman."

Julian smiled at her accusation. His hand left her chin to stroke the burning surface of her cheek.

"That's better, Emma." Once again his voice told her he expected her to remember what he was telling her. It struck her like a trainer breaking a mare to wearing a saddle—stern, yet gentle, and the trainer always made sure the mare understood who the master was. Her temper raged against that idea but her body quivered as it anticipated the demands Julian might make of it.

"Does it matter, Emma? Right here, if we shed all of these fashionable ideas and just be what we are? I was reared to act as the perfect gentleman just as you were schooled to be the image of ladylike perfection." Julian frowned at his own ideas as his eyes traced her lips and hunger flared back to life in his topaz eyes. Emma felt her mouth go dry as she felt the need to feel his kiss. It was so forbidden yet so keen. Julian's words simmered with a temptation that beckoned to her.

"Beneath it all we are flesh and blood, Emma. Society always tries to control it but that changes nothing. I want to taste you, and right here what does it matter if I kiss you? You are not a child, or a virgin, so whom do we hurt if we indulge our desire?" Julian leaned forward until his breath hit her lip. "You aren't frightened, Emma, are you? Your body is shivering with excitement. I can see it in your eyes."

His mouth landed on hers a moment later. Emma pulled away from the pure overabundance of the sensation, an involuntary twitch that she neither thought about nor controlled. Julian's hand cupped the back of her head to hold it steady as he pressed their mouths together. It was a hard kiss. Julian demanded entry to her mouth and Emma couldn't find any shred of will to resist. The tip of his tongue slipped down into her mouth, making her twist against his body once more. Her nipples instantly came alive with sensation. They were still drawn into tight little buttons that were now ultra-aware of the hard chest she was being held against. The grip on her bottom tightened as Julian's tongue thrust deeply into her mouth and stroked her own. Emma moaned as images of his cock thrusting into her body sprang into her head. Her clit sent up a shout of agreement as she felt fluid easing down the walls of her passage. The intensity of it all combined into an inferno that shook her with its strength. A whimper rose from her throat as Julian lifted his mouth from hers. He held her for a long moment as he stared into her eyes. It was a warning to remind her that he did not have to release her if he chose not to. A second later Emma was free and she stumbled back as her body felt as though it could not stand on its own without the strength from Julian's body.

"What do you want from me, sir—Julian?" He nodded approval at the use of his name and Emma frowned at her own compliance. She should not care for his good opinion but she could feel the authority radiating from him. She might refuse to bend to his dictates but this man would impress his will on her and that promise excited her further. Emma stepped away from him and the power the man seemed to wield over her body. Her will had crumbled in the face of their strange reaction to each other and she needed space to regain her composure.

"You, Emma. The terms are up to you but I intend to have you in my bed. Decide what manner of legalities you want but my intentions are very basic." Julian offered her a bow before he aimed that hard determination at her once again. "Husband, lover, friend—choose whichever suits you best but I will have you."

She turned and escaped. Julian growled as he forced his boots to stand in place. He only moved to ensure that he might watch her until she arrived at the house. Instinct refused to allow him to take any chances with her safety; in fact, Julian would have enjoyed any excuse to fight at that moment. His blood raged with need as his cock throbbed for satisfaction. The idea of fucking a willing maid only further angered him. The slightest scent of Emma's pussy had teased his nose and Julian knew that he was ruined forever when it came to other females. His cock craved Emma just like his mind did. It was a decision that rose up from the darkest corner of his character. It was born in that place that teachers and parents had never touched. That deep and often disliked place where a man was forced to confront his true nature. Lust rolled from that source like smoke from a fire. Even marriage sounded good because it would prevent any other man from touching Emma. Julian growled as he thought about her first husband, the thought of any man getting between her thighs enraged him. The idea that she belonged to him was growing so rapidly there was no stopping it. The only thing Julian might control was the speed with which he pressed Emma to accept him. Julian turned and moved toward the stables. He needed hard work to keep his hands off what he truly craved. Emma wasn't ready for him yet and there were some things that might be hurried but not rushed. She needed time to understand the heat building in her own body. His kiss would linger in her mind as her pussy refused to be content in her cold bed. Human or horse, there were similarities that could not be denied. Julian had learned that fact long ago—when a man was pressed he would revert to his true nature.

It was the same with a woman. Emma wanted him, she could no more alter that fact than he might. It was something that was born deep inside both their bodies, that flash and recognition of a superior mate. The animals were just a bit more honest about it all. A mare never let herself be mounted by a stallion she didn't approve of—that was the same quality that attracted him to Emma. She was tossing back all the weakling gentlemen her father paraded in front of her because she wanted to see if any of them would muster the courage to attempt to corner her.

Julian took a deep breath and still caught the scent of Emma's pussy lingering in his senses. Just tiny bits, but his cock twitched in response. He turned to look back at the house. He was brutally honest, and it was a tenet of his personality that often saw him keeping company with stallions instead of friends.

But he would have Emma, and Julian knew that the chase was going to be as much fun as the ride.

WHAT SHE WANTED? EMMA heard those words bouncing about inside her brain as she tried to force her legs into a calm stride. There was nothing peaceful happening in her body just then. Her heart pounded and her blood raced through her veins as her passage yearned. Hunger gnawed at her for something that she really was not certain of . . . only that she needed it so much, she was willing to listen to Julian's words.

She shouldn't. Somehow, she should be able to ignore his carnal suggestions just as she often advised Annabelle to do. But her body was making it impossible. The tops of her thighs were wet with fluid that eased from her passage. Emma pressed a hand to her mouth as her lips tingled with delight from that kiss. Her nipples joined the rest of her flesh in their wanton response to Julian as she hurried toward her room and the sanctuary it offered.

But the second Emma closed the door she found that the true cause of her dilemma was locked in that room with her. There was no way to run from her own body.

That was such a curious thing. Emma moved toward her mirror and looked at her face. Her lips were rosy red and her cheeks flushed with color. She had never seen herself looking so . . . wanton. It was strangely attractive. Her face was alight with life and there was a part of her that rejoiced in the freedom to display her passions so vividly. Her gaze caught the reflection of her bed as her passage gave another twist. She hated the very idea of lying among the bedding alone. She wasn't even in bed and Emma knew by looking at it that it was cold.

Her memory ignited with the image of Herbert fucking Tellie. Emma turned to stare at her bed as she recalled the details of the way his cock had worked between her spread thighs. Her own feet moved farther apart as the folds of her sex felt swollen and too crowded. The thought of lying back on the bed with her legs wide simmered with dark temptation because Emma knew it would relieve the ache between her own thighs.

But not completely. Emma suddenly clearly understood what her body was demanding. Her passage wanted to be fucked exactly like Tellie had been. The image of Julian holding her pressed down onto her bed stole her breath as a little whimper escaped her lips. That throbbing at the front of her sex increased its intensity as hunger twisted her into a knot so tight, it was becoming painful.

Lover.

Dare she? Would she finally understand what caused the other ladies to sigh and cast dewy eyes at their favored gentleman? Oh, it was such a dark idea but one that taunted her with the possibilities of pleasure. For the first time ever she want to have a cock inside her. Not any cock. Emma craved Julian to be the man thrusting into her, holding her solidly in place as he made his demands on her body. There was no other male she would allow or accept. More heat flickered to life in that spot at the front of her sex as she turned back around to look at her face. The clear certainty of her hunger flickered in her eyes as she felt her sex throb for what her fantasies tempted her with. It was not a matter of deciding anything, it was a moment when she understood what her flesh craved. Right or wrong was not part of the pulsing storm sweeping aside every well-thought-out plan she had in place for her life. This was a moment when Emma looked into her mirror and saw her truest nature looking back at her.

She need do nothing about it at all. She might avoid Julian and be content with her lot. The yearning inside her passage might burn her to death and yet she could refuse Julian.

If she were a coward, that is.

Emma smiled at her reflection as she lifted one hand and tugged her glove free. She traced her lower lip with the tip of a naked finger and smiled wider at the sensation that shot across her skin in response. It was like discovering buried treasure, her body was alive with pleasure and temptations that promised deeper delights. Coward? She certainly was no such thing!

Yet that did not mean Julian would have his way with her. Emma pulled her glove back on and patted her hair before turning toward the door. Julian Stanley had another thing coming if he thought he had put her in her place!

Emma was going to enjoying ensuring the man understood that she was mistress of the house and quite able to face him down.

Excitement raced through her body as she entered the hallway and Emma laughed at it. This was one summer party she was growing very fond of.

Buried treasure had never intoxicated any man as much as it was doing to her.

THREE

EMMA KEPT HER PRACTICED smile on her face. Oh, but she did not want to! Standing in the ballroom once again, she was tapping her foot beneath her skirt as the music rose to a quick tempo. She harbored a deep affection for dancing. That trait was rather misplaced in her façade of longing for her dead husband, so she was condemned to stand aside as the rest of her father's guests took to the center of the floor.

Oh, curse and rot it all! It was enough to tempt her into sailing for one of the tropical islands where rumor hinted at a life filled with scandalous disregard for propriety. Places where natives didn't even wear clothing in the warm tropical sun. Emma pressed her lips tightly together as the urge to giggle threatened to break free. No doubt, half the good wives in the room would collapse if they knew she was thinking about bare-breasted Indians frolicking on the sandy beaches.

But even darker images danced through her mind. Those same natives mated whomever they desired. Even so far as to have a husband and lovers. Her nipples tingled as she considered a place where answering the cry of your flesh was not considered a sin. What an intriguing idea to think that sex might have no value beyond the enjoyment you gained from it. Ideas like duty and chore would never be linked to it. That left so many possibilities that all brought her back to the way Julian had kissed her. The temptation of his words that they might escape and only care about their own desires simmered in her thoughts as it tried to rise above the taboos she had always been taught to respect.

"Will you dance with me?"

The invitation was unexpected, so much so that Emma turned too quickly and had to step back because the owner of that husky voice was so close to her. She tipped her head back as she stared at Julian. Her brain instantly identified his voice, almost as if she'd known him for decades instead of hours. Heat flashed across her face as Emma recalled how much better she did know Julian than most of the gentlemen she'd known for decades. Intimate details that she had never even considered wondering about. Such as the warm scent of his skin. She had smelled it as he kissed her and even now it teased her nose, like some sort of secret between them.

"Forgive me, sir, yet the dance is half past."

"What does that matter when I can see your slipper keeping time with the violin?"

Emma gasped, but caught the little sound inside her mouth because Julian was watching her with his topaz eyes once again. Her newly constructed confidence crumbled like sand, leaving her prey to the emotional tide that had left her running for sanctuary earlier. She might like to believe she could hold him at bay, but the reality was the way her nipples were hardening just because he was looking at her breasts. The reaction was instant and beyond her control, leaving Emma biting her lower lip as she hesitated to allow him any closer.

"We might disrupt the dance set."

One corner of his mouth lifted as his hand rose and moved closer with its open-palm invitation. "I believe I disrupt you."

Emma felt her blood race through her veins in the face of such boldness. She really shouldn't have felt that way and yet she did. It shocked her and excited her both at the same time. Her hand landed on his gloved palm as she watched the simmer of some carefully controlled flame in those topaz eyes. Lurking behind his stern expression was something that made her shiver.

Julian pulled her away from the wall the second their gloved hands touched. His fingers closed around hers in a solid grip that felt very much like a trap snapping on a foolish rabbit that had let its hunger lure it too close.

They joined the lines of dancers as Emma forced her brain to stop concocting such fanciful ideas and focus on the steps of the dance. Her partner brushed behind her as the tempo allowed and her skin tingled again as she felt him close to her back. It was such a suggestive thing, knowing he was going to pass behind her but having to stare straight ahead as the steps of the dance allowed him to move. Emma had never once felt so aware of her partner, her breath moving too quickly as she tried to calm her racing heart.

For heaven's sake, she knew little more than his name.

And yet she was more aware of him than she could ever recall being of any person she had ever known. It made no sense. Tossing all control aside was foolish as well as dangerous. The man might take her body and soil her name on his way out the door. Emma shivered as she caught all the eyes on them, the busybodies taking notes as Julian partnered her through the steps of the dance.

"Do you truly care what the gossips might say?" Julian whispered his question as he passed behind once again. Emma lowered her eyelashes as she looked to the floor to try and find him.

She couldn't hear his polished boots as they moved behind her across the wood floor. For such a large man, he appeared to handle his frame perfectly. Very much like a predatory hunting feline, the kind that preyed on the herd roaming the African savanna. Those lions were large but full of grace. They were deadly polished hunting machines.

"Your eyes say you do not, Emma."

Emma found her lips trying to twitch upward again. Bold suited Julian well. The music reached its zenith and she turned to drop a deep curtsy toward her partner. Emma didn't look down though, she dipped her chin due to years of training by strict governesses, but her eyes looked up to find those topaz flames.

"Your eyes say a great many things. I confess I enjoy them overly much." Julian considered her face a long moment as Emma recovered from her curtsy. "Will you take a turn about the grounds with me?"

"Indeed, sir! You are very bold." A stroll through the garden was best suited to young sweethearts. "I am a widow." Emma forced her words to be firm. A little twist of fear was eating away at her earlier delight in the way her body responded to Julian. There was her family to consider as well and it felt as though every pair of eyes in the room was on them.

"Your heart is no more chained to a grave than I am interested in any of these ladies of society." Hard determination blazed from his eyes as his face offered her a stern expression. In its way, Emma found more honesty in that hard mask than all the practiced smiles surrounding her. Julian was no dandy, foolish boy. The hard maturity of a man stared at her as Julian refused to be brushed aside with polite niceties. He saw right through her and another ripple of excitement shook her. She should have been angry, but instead her heart accelerated.

He suddenly swept her a practiced bow and this time her ears heard the distinct click of his boot heels hitting each other. He recovered quickly and just as fast his hand had curled around hers and brought it to rest on his forearm. Julian turned neatly on one heel and was escorting her from the room before her gasp escaped her lips.

"Again, I must offer the question, do you truly care what any of these overspoken gossips think?" His eyes moved to look at her as his hand stayed firmly in place over her fingers. It felt very much like a dare. Emma frowned at him but Julian did not give her time to debate her compliance. The cool night air slapped against her warm face as Julian swept her through a set of double French doors that stood open.

"I confess I don't much care if they think to comment on our escape. Besides, I already asked you to marry me so what is there for the old crows to say?"

Emma yanked her hand from his grasp. He frowned at her as she firmly clasped her hands together in front of her body and took several quick steps away from his body. There was a certain comfort in believing she was beyond his reach but a second look at his large body told her Julian would not find it difficult to renew his grip on her if he wanted to. The grin sitting on his lips surprised her, shocking Emma with the knowledge that her abrupt and even possibly rude action had struck Julian as amusing.

"I have agreed to nothing." Emma felt another twist of excitement move through her as an image of a wedding night with Julian flashed into her brain. "I do not know you."

Emma watched the way Julian positioned his body so that she would have to venture too close to him once more in order to enter the ballroom. Julian was still grinning just a tiny amount as he stepped toward her and Emma moved back from the threat of his body.

"All the more reason for us to become lovers."

Her face turned scarlet in response. Julian's hand snaked out and lightly stroked her cheek. "Lovers are the most intimate of companions, Emma. There will be nothing I would refuse to teach you about myself."

"What do you want, sir? I assure you I am not some light tumble if that is upon your mind. Marriage is not a game." Emma lifted her chin and ordered her feet to stand firmly in place—Julian had been steadily backing her into the shadows cast by the garden plants. Her nipples were actually tightening into little hard buttons as, due to distance, the sounds of the night took precedence over the music in the ballroom. She shivered as she recognized Julian was moving her farther away from any eyes that might wander onto them. A wave of vulnerability engulfed her as that flicker of excitement stoked the fire in her lower body once again.

Julian sighed before he clasped his hands behind his back and stopped moving toward her. "For many, marriage is a game." Dozens of mothers in the ballroom would be instructing their unmarried daughters to move into his path now that his name was known. They coveted his title and money and it was as serious a game as any gambling.

"There is yet another reason I would not hesitate to stand up beside you, Emma. It has been a very long time since I encountered a woman who didn't see me as a fortune instead of a man."

His words sounded sincere and they calmed her racing heart. Yet it did not alter the aggressive edge to his bold words; it felt like he was herding her into place. Like a stallion did to a mare once he'd selected her. Julian cast a look back at the crowded dance and his lips pressed into a hard line. Emma stared at the expression as understanding washed over her. The distorted and exaggerated social interactions taking place back at her father's ball were completely repugnant to him. Instead he really did have more in common with a lion—he'd cut her from the rest of the group, quickly and efficiently. Yet that did not make it a wise place for her to remain.

"Should I have reason to covet your money?"

One dark eyebrow rose as Julian considered her. "I am Herbert's brother."

Julian watched for her reaction and the distaste that shone in her eyes pleased him immensely. "Our father has become rather distressed over the fool's conduct and sent me to ship my little sibling home."

Emma giggled, she simply could not help herself. "Oh my, I believe I understand your disdain for the ballroom, Julian." And she did. It was clear that Julian was older, so in line to inherit far more. The poor man would be pursued like a fox on hunting day once word circulated among her father's guests.

Julian lifted one hand and held it up in another invitation. "You have no more desire to stand among the hopeful gold diggers than I do. Since we've escaped, let us not discard our opportunity to please ourselves."

"Indeed." *Please themselves?* "You are boldness incarnate." But Emma heard her own voice and it wasn't as stern as it should have been. Excitement laced the sound and Julian's mouth lifted in response.

"Perhaps I am, lady. But I am honest."

A little gasp left her throat as Emma stared at the temptation Julian embodied. He truly was exactly that—honest. So much so, Julian did not even bother to don the mantle of expected social party attendance in order to meet her. His approach was far more . . . primitive. What shocked Emma the most was the ripple of anticipation that idea unleashed in her own body. A jolt of sensation traveled over her skin and down into that throbbing place between her thighs. It was not a reaction to polished words or manners, her body was trying to gain more attention, and that blunt fact shocked her.

"I only came to meet you, Emma. Call me bold, yet you will never have reason to label me fickle."

Emma smiled at that idea. No, she could agree with Julian on that point. A woman would never question just where she stood in this man's affections. Julian would ensure you knew directly as well as very bluntly how he felt.

"Now that, Emma, is exactly why I want to be your lover." Julian let his eyes move down her body in a slow viewing of her form. Emma was quite sure he wanted her to know what he was about and her cheeks warmed with a blush at the pure carnal nature of the moment. His eyes rose back to hers as Julian took another step toward her. Emma held her ground and she had to raise her chin to hold their gazes on each other. Her nipples tingled beneath her dress as she became deeply aware of how much larger Julian was as opposed to her. Julian considered her face a moment. "You are a delight, Emma." He closed the distance between them with one lightning-swift step and his fingers brushed down the side of her face. His skin was sinfully hot in contrast to the night air.

Words failed her as Emma still felt the stroke of his hand. Her cheek was acutely aware of the fact that Julian had removed his glove and touched her with his bare skin. It felt so wicked to know he'd shucked the little invention of society the second they were hidden from the curious eyes of her father's guests.

"Beauty is an overused word that often only lands on a lady if she is connected with the correct people. Delight on the other hand is a state of being that you have managed to raise in me with the fire I see burning in your eyes. It is more than flesh, Emma, it is rooted in your spirit and born from the fiber of your character. What is the color of your hair compared to that? Absolutely nothing as far as I am concerned."

Julian lifted his ungloved hand once again and Emma felt her skin shiver with anticipation. She watched those fingers come closer but did not turn her face away. She couldn't find the strength to forbid herself that pleasure now that she knew how much she had enjoyed it. The tips of his fingers stroked her face from her jaw to her cheekbone and then he cupped her face with his entire hand. Sensation raced down her body and Emma felt her nipples tingle. It was such a forbidden thing to notice but both her nipples kept tightening into hard little buttons. The current fashion of light corset meant her breasts were not laced down tightly; instead they were gently supported. But a lady simply didn't spend so much time noticing her breasts.

"Enough talk." Julian moved suddenly and Emma found her body captured against his. He pulled her against his frame and even cupped the cheek of her bottom to press her hips toward him. Her breath froze in her chest as her body erupted in a storm of heat. Her nipples begged to be free from her clothing so that they might be even closer to him. Julian held her with one arm and cupped her chin in his free hand. He raised her face until his topaz eyes were burning into hers once again. Her will wanted to crumble in the face of his determination but Emma let her temper rise up to defend her will. She would not be tumbled so easily!

"I want you to think about my kiss every second that you run from me and yourself. Desire isn't something you plan, it strikes like a snake and once it's flowing through your blood, you will succumb."

Emma gasped and Julian took instant advantage. His mouth captured hers and his tongue thrust deeply into her open mouth. He stroked her tongue with his and Emma indulged her need to stroke his tongue in return. There was no need to consider her actions when it felt so good to kiss him back. Her hands spread out over his chest and she let her fingers stray under his overcoat. His chest was covered in thick muscles that delighted her. The idea that he was so strong sent more heat pouring down into her passage. Emma actually felt fluid easing over the tops of her thighs once more as Julian thrust his tongue deeply into her mouth, and her passage ached to be filled.

Julian broke the kiss as he caught the scent of her arousal. He was a man who prized his control, but the smell of her wet pussy was testing the limits of his restraint. Dark ideas of pressing her back into the darkness and spreading her thighs made him clench his teeth against the demands of his cock. He wanted to fuck her so badly it burned away every principle he held, leaving him with nothing but the need to make sure Emma would welcome him back after the first fucking.

"I know you are not an easy tumble, Emma, but I am going to get inside you. Very soon." Emma shivered against his chest because she was suddenly so very aware of how simple it would be for Julian to take what he wanted. Her body was slight compared to his and her hands were resting on the hard proof of how strong his body was beneath the carefully tailored trappings of gentle society.

Yet Emma knew there was nothing remotely tame about him. He was a predator that blended into the surroundings in order to be a more effective hunter. His cock was hard against her belly, telling her exactly what he wanted from her.

To mate. Stripped down to its most basic form, that was the

truth. It did not shock her. Instead Emma felt her clit pulse with need as more fluid coated the tops of her thighs. Her body was in direct conflict with her carefully decided plans. At that moment there was a large part of her that secretly wished Julian would take his kill without any further delay. A dark image of her thighs spread wide by his hips made her clit ache for it to become reality.

"Maybe you are more ready than I think." Julian's voice was a deadly whisper as he leaned down next to her neck. Emma heard him inhale deeply next to her skin before he growled softly. "I can smell your heat. Did you know that, Emma? The tops of your thighs are wet and I can smell it."

"Julian." Emma had no idea if she muttered the word in outrage or delight. The two emotions were twisted together so tightly, she could not tell them apart.

"I'm going to be your lover, Emma. Make no mistake, you belong to me." Both his hands clasped her bottom as he used his fingers to rub each rounded curve. It was the most blatant touch she had ever felt. But his possessive words demanded a denial as Emma fought to maintain some shred of her own personality.

"I will be no man's toy."

"And still, I will play with you." Julian's eyes blazed with determination and then he lifted her up his body. Emma whimpered as Julian used his grip on her bottom to pull her right up his length. Her thighs spread instantly as he pressed her toward his body as he lifted. A bare moment later, the hard bulge of his cock was pressing against her sex with only their clothing between them.

Emma moaned as need clawed through her passage. It was so great, it hurt. She felt so empty and his cock felt so hard. What did anything matter but letting Julian fill her? Something hard took her weight and her eyes flew open to notice that Julian had backed them through the hedge to the half wall that bordered the garden. He barely fit in the spot between bushes, and leaves brushed his shoulders as some of the branches unbent behind his back. He cupped her chin as her thighs were spread wide by his body. "Playing is the best part of being lovers, Emma."

His mouth captured her gasp and his tongue thrust deeply inside. Julian's hands left her bottom to smooth over her spread thighs and over her bent knees. She should have been horrified about being spread out so simply but her body screamed for more. Their clothing was too much to bear when all Emma could think about was the promise Julian had made to play with her.

Her hem went right up over her knees as Julian grasped her skirt in both hands and raised it. The cool night air brushed her thighs where her stockings ended and nothing but bare skin was revealed.

"The scent of your pussy is driving me insane, Emma." Julian tucked her skirt back as his hands landed on her bare thighs. Her body jerked in response to the skin-to-skin contact. Julian's eyes flickered right above hers as he watched her in the dark to gauge her reaction. There were so many things she might have done but nothing made it past the heat consuming her. Even the fear of being discovered didn't stand any real chance against the rising tide of need. Emma wanted more of the sensation that was eating at her, she craved to dive deeper into those dark rumors of passion that could tempt good girls to toss caution to fate as they took lovers in the darkest hours of the night.

"This is insanity." Emma's words were as much for herself as for Julian. Maybe more for her because Julian did not belong in her polished, proper world. She had noticed that the first time she looked into his eyes. This rush of sensation and wicked touching was in perfect harmony with that flicker of untamed heat she witnessed in those topaz eyes. Julian belonged right there, demanding favors that Emma had never considered granting to anyone else.

"No, Emma, this is the reality that everyone lies to cover up." His breath brushed her lips as he stroked her bare thighs once again, slowly moving his hands over the top of each limb as Emma felt the breath lodge in her lungs while she waited for him to get closer to that throbbing at the top of her sex. "It's what our flesh craves, but those fools back at your father's party label it a sin." His hands stopped a mere touch away from her spread sex. "Maybe it is, but it's one we will be damned for together."

Julian brushed her sex and her bottom jerked toward his hand. Emma frantically grabbed for his arms to keep from falling backward into the lower garden. She need not have worried because Julian snaked a hand around her hips and held her in place as his fingers brushed her spread flesh again. The wall was two feet wide but her fingers curled around his arms, refusing to part with the object she had been thinking of so much. Pleasure twisted up through her passage so intensely, Emma couldn't think. There was nothing but the burning need, and the world's opinion could be damned. Her body refused to debate anything but the desire to let Julian handle her exactly the way he wanted to.

A deep growl shook his chest as Emma opened her eyes and stared into the mesmerizing pair of topaz eyes. Those fingers moved until one single digit slid up the center of her folds. Julian dragged his finger forward until he found that spot at the top of her mons that had been throbbing. The second his fingertip touched it, her hips gave another jerk as a moan rose from her chest.

"That's the spot, isn't it, Emma? Your clit is begging for any touch—finger or cock. It just burns, doesn't it?" His finger rubbed the little button he named a clit as Emma gasped and tried to keep her cries discreet. Julian smiled at her face as he rubbed her clit once again. "Look at me, Emma." His voice was hard with authority as his finger froze on her clit. Her hips jerked toward that touch, frantic to gain more friction. With Julian's hand holding the back of her hips, and his hips spreading her thighs wide, she was powerless to control any motion. Emma opened her eyes again and stared into his. His finger moved instantly.

"Keep your eyes open. I want to watch your pleasure peak." He wanted to strip away every covering she had and view her soul. Somehow, Emma understood that she had never been intimate with anyone before that moment.

Julian's finger rubbed against her clit as she gasped and struggled to pull enough breath into her starving lungs. It was a battle to keep her eyes open. All she wanted to do was fall into the swirling abyss of sensation and pleasure. It was tightening under that single finger as Julian began to rub faster.

"Have you ever come before?"

His finger slowed down as he waited for her to answer. Emma frantically tried to make her brain find the answer to his question so that he would return to rubbing her clit faster. "I don't know what you mean."

Another growl shook his chest as Julian moved away from her clit. A whimper rose from her chest as he trailed his finger through her folds to the opening to her passage. He thrust his finger into her body, making her gasp as pleasure shot up into her belly. The walls of her passage were so empty, they tried to clamp around that finger as her hips lifted, offering her body to Julian.

"So, your husband fucked you but never took the time to make sure you enjoyed it? Were you ever this wet for him?"

"Wet?"

The confusion in her voice made Julian snarl. It was a damn selfish man who fucked without taking a few minutes to warm up his partner. It was little wonder most of the good wives in the ballroom whispered to their daughters that sex was a duty best endured while silently praying. Their husbands were lazy bastards who didn't give a damn about anything but their own cocks. Julian thrust two fingers up into her pussy and groaned at the little wet sounds he heard.

"Wet like this." His fingers thrust again and again as Emma lifted her hips for the penetration. "When your pussy is wet, it tells a man you want him to fuck you."

Emma gasped but not in shock. Every fiber in her body shouted with agreement as Julian thrust his fingers into her pussy again. Her bottom wanted to lift for his thrusts just as Tellie had done for Herbert's cock. Her hands clung to Julian's arms as she leaned back to offer her spread body to his touch. Everything was twisting into a knot that pulsed with the same rhythm as her heart rate. Julian watched her the entire time as she heard her own little pants.

"I'm not going to fuck you here, Emma."

Emma moaned. She needed so much from him at that moment. Julian pulled his fingers from her pussy and slid them up the center of her folds. His eyes flashed with warning as he rubbed her clit once again.

"I'm going to leave you hungry, Emma, but with enough of a taste to convince you to come to my bed tonight." His finger rubbed her clit as she gasped. Her body and will battled against each other as the forbidden became obsession. She wanted what she'd always been told to shun. Her body was shivering as Julian rubbed her clit faster and Emma felt her body beginning to burst. Pleasure suddenly snapped her like a leather lash. It shot up from her clit into her belly as her pussy contracted and lamented the fact that it was empty. Julian's mouth covered hers and caught the low moan that escaped as her body jerked and twisted while pleasure rippled over her. It all settled under that finger that gently rubbed at her clit. The tension was dull now but not banished. Her pussy felt so empty and unsatisfied.

"Look at me, Emma," Julian commanded her with hard authority. The raw hunger simmering in his eyes frightened her slightly. The hand on the back of her hips moved and pulled one of her hands off his arm. A second later her hand was pressed over the hard shape of his cock. Emma gasped but her fingers curled around the hard length as her pussy gave a twist of need to be filled by that hard flesh.

"Go back in and dance with your father. Then kiss him good night and let your maid tuck you in to bed. I will not fuck you on this wall for the first time."

She gasped at the raw use of the word "fuck" but Julian didn't soften his intentions. Her lips parted with astonishment but her eyes flickered with hunger. She only hesitated because he was rushing her, but Julian couldn't wait. The scent of her hot pussy was whipping his own lust into a frenzy. But he craved more than just getting his cock inside her, there was a burning need to know she lay down with him of her own will. Julian craved knowing that the same woman who had dropped her robe for Herbert would indeed welcome him into her bed. Pride was often the root of most men's failures but Julian embraced the burn of his tonight. Conquest was going to be so much sweeter when Emma took him into her body. Capturing her would be good but seducing her was going to be beyond anything he might anticipate.

Julian lifted her off the wall and her skirt fluttered toward her feet. Her legs quivered as her clit protested being pressed between her thighs once again. She hated her dress because it was too tight, and her skin was cold now that Julian wasn't stroking her any longer. Her temper rose up as Emma looked at the harsh demand sitting on Julian's face. It was more than demand, there was the promise of retribution if she did not comply with his wishes. There was a large part of her that wanted to toss his instruction to the ground, just to see if she could push him out of his firm stance.

But a shiver shook her body as Emma considered Julian taking her to task. Her eyes roamed his larger frame as she considered how helpless she could be in his embrace if he desired it. It was an odd thing to think but Emma couldn't dismiss how exciting it was to be clamped against his body. There was a part of her lurking behind her confidence that enjoyed the way Julian took what he wanted from her.

"Go, Emma."

The word "fuck" screamed through her head as her body gave a shout of approval. Her pussy twisted and demanded she forget that dance in favor of escaping the party for her bed. She was no longer interested in the crush of politeness her father's party would press onto her. No, her body wanted what Julian promised. It might be a harsh word and one most considered unfit for a lady's ears but it was the truth. Emma did not want to marry Julian and perform her duty, she wanted him to fuck her. In that mindless way that gossip hinted—true lovers sneaking away into the dark to act like primitive animals.

She was already turning before her pride sent out a denial, but it was a weak protest that never held a chance against the burning need still throbbing in her clit. Emma turned back around to look at Julian as he watched her do his bidding. Her lips pressed into a firm line as she let her eyes slide down his body to where his cock formed a bulge in his pants. Her mouth went dry as she recalled exactly how it had felt pressing against her palm. She craved to know what Julian could do to her body with his. Emma needed to understand what seemed to be beyond her comprehension about passion. She knew only one thing for certain right then—Julian was the man who could teach her what desire truly was. His touch did burn her skin and his kiss still lingered on her lips. Her nipples were hard little buttons beneath her cotton dress as she tried to control the need to pant because her heart was still racing. Was this what made the girls cast dewy eyes at the gentlemen? Somehow, Emma doubted it. This rush of sensation was deeper and darker than a mere affair of the heart. Her flesh rippled with demands that traveled into the most secret part of her midnight fantasies. It was in conflict with everything she had been reared to consider correct. Excitement poured out from her understanding of that fact. Following her desire meant embracing that part of her that was untamed by the rules set down by the people around her. It meant escaping the net that Emma saw tonight for the first time, that bound her to unnatural rules that conflicted with her own personality. There was a creature inside her, struggling to breathe, and that flicker of heat in Julian's eyes was a reflection of his own inner battle. They were kindred souls in the most animalistic manner. It really was not a decision; instead Emma realized she was looking at herself honestly for the very first time. This craving was part of who she was, and tonight she was going to shun the rest of the world as she embraced it.

"You may be my lover, Julian."

FOUR

LOVER. IT WASN'T THE victory Julian had thought it might be. Fate had a twisted sense of humor at times. His lips curved into a smile as he jumped the wall and moved through the garden. The darkness suited his mood as did the cover of blackness that would allow him to escape the coy and practiced approach of the title-hungry families in the ballroom.

Lover.

He should have been ecstatic that Emma hadn't demanded his name in return for her body. A snarl rose from his chest as Julian considered the fact that as lovers both were free to leave at any time. There were parts of him that wanted to erupt into violence at the mere idea that Emma might take a different lover sometime in the future. As her lover, he could not demand she follow him, and life would have to resume at some point. The reality of the party moving on to another estate in a few days abraded his temper with the very real possibility that Emma might not follow. As a widow she could make excuses and everyone would pat her shoulder before loading into their carriages.

But the reality of her nonvirgin state sent a wave of need through his cock. Knowing she wasn't too tight to take his cock tonight made sweat pop out on his brow. Julian shrugged out of his dress coat and flexed his shoulders. He detested the current fashion because it was tailored down to a mere inch of a man's frame, in effect trapping the arms close to the body. He'd ripped more than one dinner coat because of the insistence of the tailor to make it so tight. He'd discharged more than one tailor due to their resistance to listening to his instructions to make his clothing tolerable. The night air soothed his skin, making it bearable to wait. The scent of her pussy was driving him insane. Julian could still smell it as he found a back entrance and climbed the servant stairs. His manservant waited inside the guest chamber. Calvin was the perfect companion for him—efficient and quiet. In return, Julian made sure the man had the simple comforts he enjoyed, like honey cake and a wench who could suck cock.

"My long cape." Calvin didn't even blink as he went to retrieve the item Julian demanded. The servant understood exactly what that meant—his master was leaving again. It was his duty to understand his master's needs and never critique them.

Julian shrugged into the black wool garment as he looked at the bed.

"See to the bedding and bolt the door before you leave. I was snoring in besotted drunkenness all night." Calvin gave a half bow and a tiny smirk before he moved away on silent feet. Julian felt his cock harden painfully as he moved toward the servant hallway attached to the back of the chamber.

EMMA DECIDED SHE WAS mad as her maid undressed her. Her mind must have snapped to have her thinking she might control a man such as Julian. As the girl stripped the fabric from her skin, Emma sighed in relief. But she gasped softly as the scent of her own arousal drifted up her nude body to her nose. The tops of her thighs were slick with her own juices. It was such a carnal thing to notice but it twisted her body with even more excitement as her clit began to pulse. Her pussy felt so empty, as though she had been ignoring its yearning for years. The word "fuck" was so blunt but at that moment, it was perfect for what she craved.

A bath waited for her and Emma quickly stepped into the cool water. Every little motion felt exaggerated, just as it had on her wedding night. Emma moved the soap over her arm and little goose bumps rose up as she moved her hand over her own skin. The cool water felt delicious against her warm skin, enticing her to linger, but she didn't dare.

Julian might already be watching her from behind the curtain. Emma licked her lower lip as she stood up and took the length of cotton the maid offered for drying. She was stunned slightly by the stark difference between tonight and all the nights of her married life. Was it the label of sin that made tonight so much more exciting? Her skin protested as her nightdress fluttered over it. But Emma almost gave in to the urge to sigh as the maid pulled the pins from her hair and began to work a brush through the long strands.

Maybe it was forbidden but it was too enticing to ignore. There was a part of her that wanted Julian to be watching her prepare for him. She wanted to tempt him and tease him with the wait that was driving her insane. The desire to tug on his tail, just to see if he became even more untamed, invaded her normally controlled manner.

Emma lay back in her bed and frowned. She wanted nothing controlled or patient near her tonight! The urges running through her blood were untamed and that was what she craved to embrace. She detested her maid just because the girl was practiced and polished. Care and comfort abraded her temper as she waited impatiently for the maid to pinch the candles and quit the room.

But Emma shivered as darkness surrounded her. Always she closed her eyes and drifted off into the haven of sleep as the maid thrust the room into blackness. With her eyes open, she was so very aware of how dark the night was and how vulnerable she was. A shiver shook her body and then another as she waited for the predator she had invited into her room. At any second Julian might swoop from the dark and secure her in his grip, and she would not hear his approach, of that Emma was certain.

The bolt slid on the door and she gasped. Emma sat up straight in bed as her heart raced. Her eyes searched for Julian but saw nothing but blackness. She heard the slight tsking from him before he formed from the darkness into a shadow a mere foot from her.

"Lovers do not wear cotton sacks to bed." Julian shifted and shrugged and his bare chest was suddenly revealed as whatever he wore slipped right down his back. His bare flesh showed just a bare amount against the darkness. The bed moved as Julian left and Emma was once again alone. Her ears strained to hear any hint of what he was doing as she curled her knees back and pushed the bedding off her thighs. Her fingertips found the harsher fabric that Julian had been wearing puddle on her bed. The soft glow of a colored glass lamp sliced through the blackness as Julian moved the curtain aside and reentered the room. The tiny carriage lamp looked like a toy dangling from his huge hand because it was made to fit inside a closed carriage. The glass was red to not spook any horses on the road and it surrounded Julian with a ruby glow that did not penetrate the darkness around him.

It was perfect. Just a tiny bit of light that you wouldn't be able to see through the curtain or beneath the door. Her bed would become their personal sanctuary from the rest of the world as they stole away to indulge their bodies. Julian placed the lamp on the bedside table as he frowned at her.

"I suppose I can't rip that thing off you."

Emma gasped and then a tiny moan surfaced from her chest in response. Julian was completely serious. His eyes roamed over the buttons holding her nightdress closed over her breasts as he frowned with displeasure. The ruby glow from the lamp bathed his chest as Emma became lost in her first true look at his bare skin. Her hand lifted before she thought about it and gently stroked one of the ridges of hard muscle. All the way from shoulder to one flat male nipple. She traced the darker brown skin of that male nipple before rubbing her fingertip over the puckered tip. A groan shook Julian's chest as he tipped his head toward the ceiling and sucked in his breath through gritted teeth. The harsh sounds did far more for her confidence than any flowery words might have. Knowing she drew those reactions from his larger body confirmed that her actions were the ones that gave him pleasure, just as his touch had driven her insane out in the garden. Power surged through her as Emma rose up onto her knees and flattened both her hands on Julian's chest. His chin lowered as his eyes connected with hers.

"Stroke me, Emma." His voice was husky with demand, and his words more of an order, but one that she willingly obeyed. Her hands stroked over his chest as Emma noticed how good his body felt. It was a wonder to notice because she had already been a wife and according to everything she knew, that was the extent of sex.

Oh, but this was so much more!

"Take . . . that . . . sack . . . *off*," Julian growled through his clenched teeth. Emma shivered as she lifted her hands from his chest. She fumbled the first button because her hands shook. A twist of fear was mixing with the excitement racing through her bloodstream. Julian was so close to the edge of control, she sensed it. But there was also a part of her that enjoyed his emotional instability. A whisper crossed her mind, taunting her with what might happen if Julian took what he wanted instead of commanding her to yield it.

Julian didn't wait for her to finish her buttons. As soon as she had three separated, he hooked his fingers into her nightdress and ripped it over her head. He growled softly as Emma felt her breath freeze in her lungs. She was suddenly concerned that he might not like what he found beneath that garment. She was so in awe of his body, a fear built up in her that Julian might walk away once he viewed her nude. She was not sixteen any longer.

Julian wanted to fuck. The urge flamed up so hot, he struggled not to press her back and shove his cock deeply into her. The scent from her pussy taunted him with how wet she already was. His cock would find her pussy welcoming with hot fluid to ease his fucking.

But he wanted to look at her, too. His memory paled against the way she sat right there in front of him as bare as she had been when facing down Herbert. That silent confidence was something that endeared her to him, no covering her breast with her hands or ducking her chin. Emma had made her choice to invite him into her bed and she was a woman of her word. That inner spirit was what made him determined to bind her to him. Her attractiveness went so much deeper than the color of her hair or eyes. Strength was what the animal inside him craved. Emma radiated an aura of it, drawing him in like a raptor to a shining coin tossed onto the ground. The sparkle mesmerized the hunter just as Emma was hypnotizing him.

Her dark hair was spilling down to the sheets and her breasts were full enough to fit his hands. What the hell did the current fashion know about women? They had girls binding their chests to prevent their breasts from blossoming into perfect globes like Emma's. Julian reached forward and they filled his hands as his thumbs brushed her pink nipples. His cock raged against the pair of britches he still wore but Julian refused to lift his hands from her nipples long enough to free the erection. Emma shivered as he brushed her nipples once again and then smoothed his hands down her body. Julian dropped his eyes to her mons and growled at what he'd felt in the garden.

Every last hair had been plucked clean. With the fashion of wafer-thin cotton dresses, darker-haired ladies had to pluck their pussies or risk the curls being viewed if they stood on the wrong side of the firelight.

"Lay back, Emma." She shivered as her eyes flickered with indecision. Julian cupped her chin and took a hard kiss from her lips.

He broke the kiss quickly, almost as though it was an effort to apply even that much control. Emma could see the hunger on his face and she knew that he battled against the urge to press her down and spread her thighs. That battle endeared him to her. Her husband had certainly never bothered to fend off the need to shove his cock into her the moment the maid left. There were no kisses or tender strokes over her skin to awaken her clit as Julian was doing.

"I'm ready, Julian." Emma lay back and spread her thighs. Her clit burned for another rub as her bottom lifted toward her lover. She moved back on the bed so that she was lying on it completely.

Julian chuckled as he caught both her ankles and pulled her back toward him so that her bottom was on the edge of the mattress. He pressed her down with one hand spread over her belly. "No, you aren't." His eyes dropped to her spread pussy. "But you will be soon. Half the fun of having a lover is being played with, Emma. Have you ever watched a child with a new toy? They touch each and every part of it, rubbing the shiny new paint and investigating everything about their newest possession."

Emma gasped at the idea that Julian might handle her as a plaything. Julian used his free hand to touch her slit. He stroked a finger up the center of her folds and grinned at the slick fluid he discovered waiting there. "Were you ever this wet for your husband?"

Emma giggled, she simply could not help herself. But her amusement died as Julian looked away from his stroking of her pussy and the look in his eyes made her shiver once again. A word escaped his clenched teeth as one finger thrust up into her pussy. Emma couldn't stop her hips from tilting up for that penetration. A little moan escaped her lips as pleasure filled her. One corner of Julian's mouth rose as he worked that finger in and out of her pussy. Pride shone from his eyes as she whimpered and he added a second finger.

"I'm tempted to fuck you until you can't walk tomorrow."

Another whimper came from the idea of his large body taking possession of hers.

"But first I'm going to taste you."

In her darkest fantasies, Emma had never imagined that men placed their mouths on pussies. Her fingers hooked into Julian's hair but he pressed her belly down as his tongue lapped her spread slit. Her clit jerked as the tip of his tongue flickered over it. A deep moan came from her chest as her thighs clamped around Julian's head. He chuckled as he looked up her body.

"Like that, do you, Emma?" The tip of his tongue flicked over her clit as he used his fingers to spread the folds of her sex wide. "So do I. Your pussy might become my favorite treat. I might crave a taste of it each and every night. But I'm going to make you climax once again before I fuck you." Julian reached for his pants and undid the buttons. He reached in and pulled his cock forward. Emma stared at the erect flesh with complete devotion. She licked her lower lip as she noticed how empty her pussy was and how perfect a cock was for filling that void. Julian stroked his cock from the base to the head as she watched, and she heard him chuckle.

"It will feel good, Emma, but I will have another taste of you first."

Emma whimpered as Julian lapped her slit again. He took his time as he licked her from the opening of her pussy to her clit. Her hips jerked and bucked as he chuckled. He sucked her clit right into his mouth and she whimpered as climax began to twist her. Her fingers pulled on his hair as he sucked and used the tip of his tongue on her clit. Pleasure tore into her pussy as climax broke the tension and sent a wave of delight through her. Julian rose up over her body as she cried out and his body held her thighs wide. The head of his cock pressed against her wet pussy as he thrust slowly into her body. She was still floating on the waves of pleasure as his cock stretched her pussy. Julian stopped halfway into her body and pulled free. Emma gasped as her body screamed for complete possession. She opened her eyes to see Julian's cheek flinch as he fought the urge to thrust hard. The crisp hair covering his chest brushed her nipples as he thrust his cock back into her pussy.

"Spread your thighs wider, Emma." Julian didn't wait for her to comply, he hooked each of her legs at the knees as he pushed her legs up. Her knees ended up lying on the bed at her waist level as he stood between her thighs. Julian was still standing as he thrust his cock into her. Her pussy ached but stretched to allow the possession. A deep growl told her when his cock was completely lodged inside her. The look on his face frightened her with its intensity. His hands captured each of her hips before he looked at her face.

Their eyes watched each other as he began to move his cock in and out of her pussy. Emma could hear the wet sounds her body made as she was impaled by his flesh. Her body ached but there was too much delight to worry about how large his cock was. Her bottom began to lift from the surface of the bed exactly as Tellie had done for Herbert.

"That's right, Emma, fuck me back. Lift your pussy for my cock."

Emma moaned in response, there were no words left inside her, only sensation and pleasure. It all centered around her pussy as Julian pressed his cock deeply into her. Her bottom lifted off the bed faster as she tried to increase the pace. She wanted more friction, needed Julian to fuck her faster.

"Faster." Emma didn't know where she got the notion to voice her own demands, only that she expected Julian to do as she commanded. They were lovers and that meant the rules that governed the marriage bed did not apply to them.

"No." Julian tightened his grip on her hips as he continued his pace. His cock slipped in and out of her body in a strong rhythm that shook the entire bed. He would thrust deeply into her pussy and hold his entire cock inside her for a moment before pulling loose all the way to the tip of his cock. He would hesitate with only a bare inch inside her before giving a hard thrust to penetrate her once again. Emma shivered as she opened her eyes to see that Julian was watching his cock enter her body. His breath was harsh and heavy as she witnessed the animal she'd suspected lurked beneath his polished exterior. The untamed beast was feasting on her, claiming her as a prize in some primitive hunt where she was the prey.

"I'm going to fuck you, Emma, slow and hard." Julian forced

his cock to resist the urge to spill his seed. Her pussy was tight and hot, drowning in fluid as he made sure to thrust against her clit. Her bottom worked in rhythm with his thrusts, gaining a satisfied growl from him. Had it been a mere day since he'd first seen her? It felt like a year that he'd been trying to get inside her like this. Her breasts bounced as he fucked her and climax began to drag her into another burst of pleasure as Julian refused to join her. He needed to be inside her longer, to feel her pussy grip his cock for much longer. Emma whimpered as her hands clawed at the sheet beneath her and the walls of her pussy contracted around his cock as she cried out in delight. Julian gritted his teeth as he thrust deeply into her and then pulled free once more.

The bed and everything in the room was spinning. The only solid thing was Julian and his hard thrusts. Her nipples tightened painfully as pleasure tore into her body again but Julian still did not surrender. Emma craved that last confirmation that he was as satisfied as she was. Her pussy wanted to feel his seed as it spurted deep inside her. He suddenly pulled out of her body and moved back. She stared in fascination at the cock plainly in sight. It glistened in the ruby light with the fluid from her own pussy and yet it was still difficult to believe the thing had fit inside her.

Julian pulled his britches down his legs and dropped them. His cock stuck straight out from his body with its ruby head, and her hand was reaching for it before he finished undressing. He sucked in his breath with a hiss as her fingers slipped around the ridge that encircled the head of it. Emma closed her hand around his length and her fingertips did not meet each other. There was a slight ache in her pussy now that she was empty, and she would gladly take his cock again.

But there was another thing Emma decided she wanted to try first. Slipping over the edge of the bed, she caught her body on her feet and then knelt in front of Julian. She stroked her closed hand down the length of his cock and pulled it back up before opening her mouth to take the head just as she'd seen Tellie do.

"Christ, Emma!" The phrase was another form of primitive praise. Emma understood it as she licked the slit on the top of his cock and then opened her jaw wider to suck more of the length. Julian's hand tangled in her hair as his hips began to thrust his cock into her mouth with tiny motions. The scent of his skin filled her senses as she took his cock deeper between her lips. She had thought it would taste foul but in fact the skin was smooth and very much like his kiss. More important, her confidence soared as she heard Julian hiss and his hips thrust his cock deeper into her mouth. Watching Herbert do this to Tellie, and doing it herself were far different. She was the one in control, not being used as she had thought about Tellie when witnessing Herbert demand his cock be sucked. Emma clasped her fingers around the portion that did not fit into her mouth and Julian hissed once again.

"Lick it right under the head."

Emma let her tongue flicker back and forth on that spot as Julian grunted and moaned. She stroked the length that wasn't in her mouth as she sucked harder. Finding the twin sacs that hung from the base of his cock, she gently fingered both before closing her hand around his staff once more. Julian's entire body shuddered as his breath rasped faster between his clenched teeth. The knowledge that she was pushing him toward that spinning vortex that he had introduced her to made her lick and suck on his cock even faster.

"Enough." Julian pulled her head away by her hair and then scooped her off the floor. His chest was heaving as he placed her in the center of her bed. The bed ropes creaked as he crawled up after her and let his body cover her. Emma whimpered in delight as she felt her thighs being spread by his hips, and his hands captured each of hers, pinning them above her head. Julian stared into her eyes as he pressed his cock deep into her pussy once more. He stayed still as he caught her mouth and kissed her hard. His tongue thrust into her mouth as his hips began to move again. He thrust hard and lingered inside her body for a moment before pulling free.

"You are mine, Emma." His eyes flickered with possession as his hips increased their pace. She was helpless beneath him but that knowledge sent a crazy bolt of excitement through her as Julian fucked her harder and faster. The bed shook as he snarled and bent down toward her neck. He bit the tender skin as his hips hammered into her spread body. Climax began to twist her body as Julian gave another growl and Emma felt his seed filling her belly. Pleasure twisted her harder than before as her pussy contracted around his cock and actually milked it. Her back was straining away from the bed to make sure he was as deep as possible as Julian snarled next to the bite he'd inflicted on her neck. His fingers tightened around each of hers as their hearts thumped wildly against each other.

Emma could not have moved even to save her life. Julian's body held her down and she struggled to raise her chest enough to fill her lungs. His arms moved suddenly as he rolled and took her with him. He pressed her head onto his chest as he lay on his back in the middle of her bed.

Emma wiggled in his embrace and Julian frowned at her. The ruby light reflected off his face as he caught the back of her neck in his grasp. She was full of spirit but that included dedication to her family. Taking a lover did not fit that expectation she had of herself, but Julian wasn't in the mood to allow her to retreat from him.

"I will still meet you at the altar, Emma, if that is what you need to find peace. But you will sleep against my body without a thread between us."

Emma felt tears burning her eyelids. She pushed against his chest and Julian whacked her bottom in response. A gasp rose from her chest in shock. Julian snarled softly as he rubbed her bottom.

"Lovers share the embrace all night long, Emma, because they know sunrise is going to part them." The darkness beyond the ruby glow of their lamp looked so thick, dawn was nothing but a far-off possibility.

"I do not understand your continued marriage proposals, Julian."

He laughed at her frustration. Julian moved and suddenly he lifted her up and sat her astride his body. His hands held on to her upper arms until she balanced her body and settled into the position. It was slightly shocking because her thighs were spread and her bare pussy pressed against his lower belly. His cock rose up behind her, lying against her bottom as Julian moved his hands to cup her breasts.

"Do you honestly believe any human-created ceremony could bind me to you, Emma? I'm obsessed with you. I will stalk your every step with or without the title of husband." Julian rolled her nipples between his thumbs and forefingers. "Does that make it sound better, Emma? I am as stunned as you to discover this attraction but I cannot seem to resist your pull." Hunger flared back up in his topaz eyes as one of his hands left her breast and traveled down her body to her clit. Julian didn't hurry, he lingered over every inch of bare skin, savoring the feel of it before he gently inserted one finger between the folds of flesh that protected her clit. Pleasure shot up into her pussy as he rubbed that little button. Satisfaction appeared on his face as Emma wiggled and muttered with enjoyment.

"Ride my cock."

Julian's voice rang with firm authority as he left her clit and grasped her hips. He lifted her off his body and pushed her back so that she was poised over his rigid cock.

"Brace your hands on my chest and ride me like a stallion."

Did she dare? Emma was already pressing her hands over his chest as she felt Julian release her hips. Her thighs held her weight as Julian grasped his cock and moved the head of it to the opening of her pussy. The idea sent a surge of power that Emma had never thought to associate with sex. Always she had been on her back being mounted.

"Go on, Emma, you set the pace." Emma would have sworn Julian understood exactly what their swap in position was doing for her confidence. His eyes flickered with a battle for control and she watched him resist the need to flip her onto her back. Her thighs quivered as she lowered her body and his cock penetrated her pussy.

"Now back up." Emma lifted her body up and laughed as his cock pulled from her body. She allowed herself to go back down before the head of his cock left her pussy. Julian grasped her hips and used his hold to teach her the rhythm.

"That's it, Emma, fuck me. Show me what you enjoy." Freedom burst upon her as Emma took the challenge. She moved faster and leaned forward so that her clit gained some friction. There were so many ideas rushing into her thoughts as she treasured the moment of complete superiority. It was a gift that she had never dreamed to have.

Julian watched her the entire time. She had never felt more beautiful than she did with his eyes on her. Her bare breasts jiggled with her motions as his cock demanded free rein once more.

Julian battled against that urge as he waited for her face to tell him climax was claiming her again. He sent his finger into her pussy folds once more to rub her clit and she whimpered as her rhythm became faulty. Emma watched his teeth clench as he tried to control his need to press her onto her back before she climaxed. It was a tender thing to see his attention on, because Julian took notice of her pleasure and not simply his own.

"Take what you crave, Emma." Julian's words were pure sin. They tempted beyond all control and Emma was a willing consort to him. She tightened her knees around his hips as he rubbed her clit in the same rhythm as she rode his cock. She could feel her pussy tightening around his cock like a hand trying to milk it. Julian rubbed her clit faster as she cried out and pleasure twisted her into a knot. Julian growled beneath her and flipped her onto her back a second later. His hips thrust hard as pleasure rippled through her. Julian snarled above her as he buried his cock in her pussy and she felt that spurt of his seed once again. Her body was nothing but a limp rag, so riddled with sensation, all she could do was cling to her lover as his seed filled her. Julian caught his weight on his bent elbows. His arms were on either side of her face as he brushed her lips with a kiss.

"I should warn you, Emma, I have discovered a craving for you that I fear I am going to bother you with every chance I get." His eyes flashed with determination as he turned and rolled onto his back. His arms clasped her to him as the bed jiggled with their movements. "I am going to fuck you every chance I can."

Julian pressed her head onto his shoulder as Emma tried to find some protest to his brash words. Instead she let her eyes fall shut as she realized that her own body wanted him to do exactly what he wanted with her. Contentment surrounded them along with the ruby glow from the lamp, and for that moment, everything was exactly perfect. What did it matter that there were plenty of people sharing her father's roof who would brand her scarlet for her cravings? Julian was her companion in hunger, so it fit that they shared their stolen moment of ruby-bathed peace.

Emma felt a smile lift her lips as she rubbed her hand over the crisp hair on Julian's chest. Didn't everyone agree that humans were imperfect? Somehow, she simply did not see the reverend appreciating her using that particular aspect of scripture to console her morality as she lay with her lover.

And yet she found it ever so fitting!

Julian listened to Emma's breathing slow. She slipped into slumber as he trailed his fingers through her hair. Temptation taunted him with the idea of just staying exactly where he was. He could force the issue by being found in her bed. Marriage had never appealed to him so much, and to be blunt, all he cared about was making sure no other man got his cock anywhere close to her. He curled his lips back and grinned—more precisely, he wanted the right to tear apart any man who even tried to touch her. It was a burning need that was seeping into every layer of his being. Julian was stunned to feel it taking over when he'd never been possessive of any woman before. It wasn't something that made sense. But it was as solid as stone and unwilling to be swept aside even by the satisfaction biting into his cock. Fucking her should have been enough.

It wasn't.

FIVE

EMMA WOKE AS JULIAN left. She lifted her eyelashes just as the ruby glow from the lamp was dissipating through the curtain. The bed linens were tucked around her but she was suddenly so cold and acutely aware of how alone she was. Her heart twisted as she felt tears prick her eyelids.

She might have gone her entire life without understanding. Emma felt two tears slide down her face as she looked around the dark room. A shiver shook her as she noticed the chill more than she ever had before. Her stolen moment was past and it left behind a bitter, empty pit in her heart.

Certainly, she was acting foolishly. She knew so little about Julian. Her body shivered again, protesting her logic. There were things she understood about Julian that no amount of courtship games might have taught her. Maybe that was the true difference between lovers and spouses. This deep understanding of who they each were beneath the layers of rules and social etiquette they had both been schooled in since birth.

Yet, dare she taste any more? Julian was temptation incarnate, the sort that became an addiction so powerful, you couldn't stop even to save your own sanity. After just one night she was cold.

Her bed unwelcoming in the face of knowing what it had been like to share it with Julian.

Emma kicked the covers aside, crossed the room and pulled the curtain away from the window. The horizon was pink but she didn't enjoy watching the sunrise this morning. She frowned at her own melancholy mood. To think that she had been most content just yesterday morning, and now that bliss was shattered after one night of forbidden pleasure. Her clit flickered to life softly between her thighs as her mind offered up memories of twisting desire that had bound her to Julian last night. Looking back at her bed, Emma still saw the ruby glow that had encased her with her lover like some scarlet confession.

And yet, she was not ashamed.

No, it was far worse than that. She was afraid. Julian radiated too much power, there was no controlling it. She was the kindling that burst into flame when he touched it. While she understood so much more about how the heart might lead other girls to offer up their bodies, there was something she had learned that shook her composure to its foundation.

She had no defense against Julian. Affection had already taken root in her and was sprouting into the chains that she had deceived the rest of the world into thinking bound her. Only this love wasn't for the man who had wed her but for the one she had willingly invited to become her lover.

Her pussy began to heat as Julian's image filled her thoughts. Emma resisted the hold he held on her even now when she was alone. Julian was not a man to linger at summer parties. He would disappear just as soon as he had sated his hunger between her thighs. She put no true belief in his offer of marriage because Julian had been very clear. He had wanted to fuck her and left the terms of their relationship in her hands. Emma sighed as she went searching for her discarded nightdress. She pulled the cold fabric over her head and hugged it to her chilled skin. She was grateful Julian had given her the choice. At least she didn't need to face life as an unwanted wife, used and discarded for all the world to see. But she wasn't strong enough to continue. Even one more night and she might be willing to follow Julian anywhere, casting her pride aside in favor of gaining his attention even a morsel at a time.

No, she had her sister and father to consider. The sordid gossip that would taint Annabelle if she followed her reckless passion any further. Well, as a lover she had the power to end their engagement. Moving back across the floor, Emma pushed the curtain aside and secured the braided rope that was used during the day to hold the heavy fabric to the side of the window. Dawn was casting its light across the garden now, putting an end to the night's dark allure. Without shadows to hide among, harsh reality stung as Emma sat at her desk and lifted her quill.

All love affairs had to end.

"SURELY YOU CAN PUT off your visit for another few days."

Emma bit into her lip as she let her father fluster. He peered at her through his spectacles and frowned deeply as he took in her spencer jacket already buttoned over her dress.

"You do not need me, Father. The house is full and the staff well trained to see to everything. Aunt Trudy has been all alone since your guests arrived. I will go and share the rest of the week with her. Think of how much she will enjoy company."

Her sire melted as he held out his arms for her to come forward for a hug. Emma smiled as she was embraced and her father placed an approving kiss onto her cheek.

"Such a fine daughter you are, Emma! Always thinking of the family. You tell Trudy I'll be by to see her as soon as the week is over."

"I will, Father."

Emma picked up her satchel and left. Oh, she was running and knew it well but engaging an enemy as strong as Julian was foolish. Her pride might be urging her to stand until she was forced to bend but she knew it would be a hopeless battle. So she left. It was not a question of rightness. Emma walked past the garden wall and shivered as she felt her nipples tingle. There was no resistance in her, so her only hope was to escape. Maybe it was not a grand ending to her love affair, yet it would be effective. She frowned as she moved over the pastures that separated her father's estate from his sister's. There was more to her leaving than just the fear that Julian might overwhelm her. She was filled with a deep sense of unfairness about the whole thing. Julian was not a toy and she could not shake the feeling that she was playing with him like a spoilt child who had no real care for his emotions.

Oh, now she truly had entered into the realm of tender-hearted foolishness sweeping through the women of her era! There was nothing soft about the man who had been her lover last night. Her breath caught in her throat as her pussy gave a twist of need. Those stolen hours inside her bedroom were going to live in her memory forever. Emma truly was happy about it, too, but she could not face Julian again knowing that she had invited him into her bed as if it was some manner of game. Maybe that was the current fashion, but in the harsh light of day, her cheeks stung with a blush of shame for treating something so deep in so light a manner.

She simply could not continue. Julian was worth so much

more than stolen moments and controlling words. Her own tender feelings were as well. Emma lifted her feet faster as she filled her lungs with the morning air. All things in life ended too soon except for the things you hated, and those dragged on endlessly. Lovers always parted, it was only a matter of time.

JULIAN TIPPED HIS HEAD back and laughed. The two men who had stood about attempting to help him with his stallion retreated because it wasn't a friendly sort of laughter. The sound filling the stable was full of a promise of retribution.

Julian tucked Emma's letter into his vest before he swung up onto the bare back of his mount. He gripped the beast between his thighs and grinned at the astonished looks being cast at him from the stable hands. Yes, he was unconventional. More bluntly, he was a beast and enjoyed it!

Turning toward the door, he dug his heels into the sides of his mount and gave Caesar free rein. The stallion charged out into the morning, stretching out his long legs.

A long skirt was in sight and Julian knew it was Emma. His instincts told him it was her as he leaned low over Caesar's neck. Julian curled back his lips and enjoyed the bit of lust that surged through him as he bore down on his prey. His cock stiffened until it was hard enough to hurt as Julian contemplated Emma's formal letter.

She had broken with him, so that meant the next stage of their "engagement" would be under his terms.

Julian chuckled against the stallion's neck as he gained ground on Emma.

Emma would be the one yielding to his rules now and that pleased the hell out of him!

Emma heard the approaching horse and knew instantly that it was Julian. The back of her neck tingled as she turned despite her firm resolution to ignore him. There was no controlling her body as she felt him bearing down on her like a hawk. She turned out of that same instinct a mouse did—self-preservation.

Julian truly was a beast. Emma witnessed it as he blended in perfect harmony with his stallion. The creature was black as soot and a good two hands taller than any stallion her father had ever owned. That only added to the overwhelming presence of its master.

Emma shivered. Julian was a man who could master others. She knew that, and had felt it last night. She stepped back as he reined in his mount and swung off of his mount in one powerful motion. Displeasure shone clearly on his face as he wrapped the reins around one large hand.

"Running, Emma?"

It was harsh to hear her actions spoken aloud. Fear twisted through her as Emma faced the reality of what she had awoken knowing. Julian knew her too well. It was deeper than the passion they had burned in last night, even darker than the pleasure of their colliding flesh. Julian could touch her very soul. Any manner of defense fell aside as she caught his scent and her pussy contracted with the need to once again be stretched on his cock.

"I need to—"

Julian stepped closer and Emma saw his nostrils flare slightly. "You need me, Emma, and I crave you. Do you think I enjoy it more than you? This unstoppable need that has only your face attached to it? Did you somehow convince yourself that I control it any better than you do? Fate is a bitch when she applies her whim to us mortals." Frustration flared up in his topaz eyes as Julian moved closer, and his stallion snorted as it was pulled forward by Julian's grip on the reins. But what made Emma shiver again was the determination that flared as Julian stepped up and loomed over her.

"Your note informed me that our love affair is ended."

Her throat went dry and her pussy ached in response to Julian's understanding of her message. Her clit begged for another touch, just one more possession before she barred Julian from her life.

"Good. Now you shall bend to my whims concerning our relationship."

Julian moved like lightning. He released his hold on his mount for a bare moment as his arm snaked out to capture her body. Emma shrieked as her feet left the ground and her body was weightless. She landed over the stallion's back and noticed that Julian had not even bothered to saddle his mount. She was lying across the wide shoulder of the horse with her legs on one side and her head hanging over the other. Her bottom was facing the sun as Julian swung up onto the animal's back. He dug his heels into the sides of the beast and motion was instant. He pressed his hand into her back as the stallion picked up his hooves.

It would be simple to believe Julian insane but Emma knew that he was not. No, she had taunted him with her rejection, cast a gauntlet at his feet and dared him to take what he wanted.

Julian was beast enough to answer her challenge.

SIX

HER HEAD WAS BOBBING with the pace of the stallion. Emma clung to the only thing she could and that was Julian's thigh. He firmly stroked her upraised bottom in response. Her clit pulsed instantly as her pussy quivered. Excitement raced through her as she contemplated the effect of having no restrictions on Julian. As her lover, he had to cater to her good nature. Now he might return to cutting her from the herd like she had felt he was doing that first time he kissed her in the garden. Her note had severed the relationship he had offered on her terms. It would appear that Julian was not taking his turn as the dictator. He was riding off with her like a hunting trophy and Emma shivered once more as she considered being at his mercy.

It was strange that true fear never entered her mind. Apprehension was thick enough to choke her but she did not fear for any true harm. An insane smile crossed her face as she envisioned what her governess would think of that. Julian was dragging her away with the full intention of feasting his carnal appetite on her flesh and she did not fear for her virtue.

A hard smack landed on her bottom and she shrieked. Emma instantly tried to sit up but the motion of the stallion kept her hanging over its back with her fanny unprotected. Julian snickered above her as he smoothed a hand over her smarting bottom.

"It's time you understood who your master is, Emma. Disobedience will be rewarded with punishment." He smacked her bottom again and again. Each blow was delivered with firm control as Emma gasped. Her bottom burned but suddenly her pussy burned even more as the pain traveled into her clit and set off a pulsing need to have Julian's cock deep inside her again.

Julian spanked her once more before rubbing her smarting cheeks with a firm hand. The stallion slowed to a walk as they entered a thick area of trees. Julian leaned down and hooked an arm around her waist. He pulled her up against his body and sat her upright on the horse's back. His arm bound her to him with her back to his chest. He leaned down to her neck and laid a kiss on her skin. His mouth was so hot compared to the morning air. Emma gasped as she jerked away from him but he held her captive as he nuzzled her neck and gently bit her once again.

"Are you wet, Emma? Some women enjoy being spanked." He took a deep breath next to her skin and growled softly. "I think you are. The scent of your pussy drives me insane. I can't think beyond the need to shove up inside you."

Her pussy gave a twist as Emma became aware of how empty she felt. Julian was correct, she was wet, fluid was coating the sides of her pussy and making the tops of her thighs slick. She even caught the slightest scent of her own arousal as Julian pushed his mount farther into the woods. The civilized world was far behind them as Julian took her toward the portion of the estate that was used for hunting. Ladies rarely ventured this deep into the forest and she shivered as she recognized how completely at his mercy she was.

Julian instantly smoothed a hand over her arm in response.

Emma doubted he thought about the tender motion. He nuzzled her neck once again before lifting his head to look ahead of them. A small structure emerged from the trees, a cottage of some kind, plain but sturdy looking.

"I found this while riding yesterday. Your father bid me use it while I'm here." Julian pulled Caesar to a halt in front of the little cottage. The place had housed a gamekeeper up until the man's retirement the season before. Emma's father had been lax in replacing the man, and poachers would be hunting in the private reserve if there wasn't a man there to put a stop to it.

But it was perfect for his purposes. Julian dismounted and pulled Emma with him. He spun her free and she twirled away from him as her skirt belled out from around her feet. She turned to stare at him with eyes sparkling with excitement. She pressed her lips together in a firm line but her eyes glowed with passion despite her efforts to look prim.

Emma shivered but the reason made her frown. She was so excited her body refused to remain still. She could smell Julian's skin, and his cock had pressed into her back as they rode. Her pussy was demanding another taste of that thick rod as her clit twisted with need. Julian stroked a hand up his stallion's neck before he removed the bit and reins. The horse shook its head before it turned and snorted. Julian moved away from the beast as it lifted its front hooves off the ground and let out a cry. An answering one came from the little stable sitting behind the cottage. A sable-colored mare appeared in the door frame as she snorted and cried back at the stallion.

"You placed a mare here?"

Julian turned and closed the distance between them. He captured her body against his as his eyes held her attention. A smug grin was turning his lips up as his breath teased her lips.

"Your father asked if I would let Caesar cover one of his mares. I always oversee every mounting he does so I asked your father for use of this cottage." Julian turned her around so that she was held against his chest as she faced the two horses sniffing at each other. "Have you ever watched a stallion mount a mare, Emma? It's harsh and primitive but more honest than half the guests at your father's party would admit. Watch nature at work, Emma, I didn't tie the mare in the stall. She's free to move about but she will follow her heat and not try to escape. She might kick or bite but in the end she wants to be covered. Her pussy is hot and wet just like yours. Nothing will distract her from satisfying her need to get fucked."

Julian's voice was seductive in a wicked way. His body heat soaked into her as he held her captive against his body. His cock pressed into her back, taunting her with its hard presence as Julian nuzzled her ear just like his stallion was doing to the mare. He whispered against her ear. "So very much like us, isn't it, Emma? You broke with me just to see if I would run you to ground. Admit it." The truth in his words almost drove her insane at the possibilities. Deep down she did want to act as primitively as the mare. Emma wanted to snort and hiss at Julian just to see if he would demand she surrender. It was a manner of test, there was a part of her that wanted a man willing to take her and gain proof of her willingness by touching her body and wringing a response from it. That was such a foreign idea to discover inside her own thoughts, but Julian's abduction was pleasing her on some dark level where Emma had to confess she would enjoy it if he claimed her exactly like Caesar was doing with the mare. Reacting to the heat in her pussy and acting on the impulse to mate with her.

Oh, she was wicked! Emma couldn't even chastise herself

properly because her mouth went dry as her eyes were glued to the mating dance in front of her. The stallion snorted again as he lifted his hooves and pawed at the air. Emma gasped at the stark similarities in Caesar's approach to the mare and Julian's pursuit of herself. The stallion wanted to mount the mare and intended to let his strength be the deciding factor in whether or not the mare would allow him to cover her. A shiver shook her frame as Julian bit her neck once again. One of his hands traveled down her body to the top of her mons and pressed her hips back toward his body.

"There are some differences though. If I want you to let me mount you, I'll need to give your clit a bit of attention . . . Won't I, Emma?" Julian chuckled and Emma grinned at his humor. It was rather surprising to discover that sex might be a topic for playfulness. But her grin dissipated as Julian rubbed her clit through her thin cotton dress. His hand parted her thighs as he rubbed her mons with a firm hand. Caesar circled the mare as the mare snorted and turned in a circle also. She was taunting the larger stallion and Emma shivered once more at the way that mimicked her dealings with Julian. The fact that the mare had not taken flight said she was in heat and her protests a façade. The two horses moved around each other as Julian growled in her ear.

"He's going to mount her now. See how stiff his cock is? I know exactly how Caesar feels, the scent of your wet pussy is making it rather hard to think about anything except fucking you."

Julian's words were so socially unacceptable but they excited her even further. Emma heard her own whimper as her pussy quivered in response to that word, "fuck." Oh, she did want Julian to do exactly that to her. Hold her imprisoned against his large body as he thrust his cock up inside her. Caesar screamed and turned quicker than the mare. The stallion nipped her on the flank before he mounted her. His front legs clamped around her belly as the horse thrust his engorged cock into the mare. She tossed her head but didn't flee. Emma's breath came in little pants as she watched the hard motion of their mating. Her pussy ached for the same treatment as Julian rubbed her mons again.

"Would you welcome me, Emma? Play the mare and let me mount you?"

Oh, Lord . . . yes! Every fiber in her body clamored with agreement as a whimper rose from her throat. Her hands covered the arm holding her against Julian as Emma found her fingers stroking his forearm and relishing the strength she felt through his wool coat.

The little sound cut through the last of his control. Julian let Emma go as he reached for her skirt. He tugged twin handfuls of the skirt up as he bent forward and pushed her toward the forest floor. "On your hands and knees, Emma! Your stud is ready to mount you."

The air was cool as it hit her bare skin and Emma moaned as her hands pressed into the soft earth. Emma heard his clothing being ripped open a second before Julian grasped her hips again. Caesar was still thrusting hard into the mare as Julian's cock probed for the entrance of her pussy. He held her hips as he thrust hard into her body and Emma cried out as his cock stretched her pussy once again. Her knees slipped further apart as she raised her bottom for Julian's next thrust. Her pussy was so wet, he penetrated deeply and slid smoothly out before he gave a hard thrust to impale her again.

A smack landed on her bare bottom, making Emma gasp. Julian chuckled from behind her as he thrust his cock into her and smacked her other cheek.

"You have been bad, Emma. Breaking off with me was very

disobedient. Now you will get the touch of the whip that you so richly deserve from your master."

"I think not!" Emma tried to surge up from her prone position instead. Julian smacked her bottom quickly in response as he shoved his cock into her pussy with quick thrusts. Her pride wanted to refuse but her body wasn't willing to follow. Pleasure was tightening and twisting her into a single pulsing knot of need. Her clit screamed for friction as Julian spanked her again. The sharp sting only intensified the pleasure, making Emma lift her bottom higher for Julian's fucking.

"Admit I'm your master, Emma! Tell me your pussy was made for my cock alone." His voice was hard with need as his cock slammed against her bottom and he smacked each cheek again.

"I will not!"

Julian leaned over her body, pressing her back onto her hands and knees with his body covering hers to hold her in the submissive position. His cock was lodged deep inside as he bit her neck.

"I will be your master, Emma. Would you like me to keep fucking you? Or shall I stay still and enjoy the way your pussy grips my cock?"

Emma sobbed with need so acute it bordered on pain. She needed him to move, was desperate for relief from the hunger burning in her clit.

"I want you to fuck me." Julian pulled out of her body and thrust back inside twice in reward, but he froze again as his demand for the word "master" hung between them. Emma bit into her lip to hold back her complete surrender to him. He stroked his hands down the sides of her body as he nuzzled her ear.

"I could make you climax like this. Did you know that, Emma? All I have to do is reach around and rub your clit as I fuck you. You would come under my touch."

Emma moaned as one large hand stroked over her lower belly to the top of her sex. Julian's breath hissed next to her ear as his fingers drove between the folds of flesh covering her clit. He rubbed her clit and she bucked. Her bottom lifted for his service just as the mare was doing for Caesar. Julian pulled his cock free and thrust it hard back into her pussy, rubbing her clit at the same time, and Emma cried out as pleasure tightened around her clit. She actually shivered as she felt climax begin to break but Julian pulled his finger off her clit the second before pleasure took her.

"Master. Admit it."

Emma shook her head as she moaned for relief. Julian lifted his chest away from her back and drove his cock in and out of her pussy with a few hard motions. His hand smacked her bottom again and the little sharp blows made her frantic for his finger to return to her clit.

"One simple word, Emma. Your body understands. Do you know that's why your bottom lifts for my cock?" Julian smacked her bottom and thrust hard into her pussy. Emma felt her bottom rise without any consideration from her. She even pushed back toward his thrust as a little cry of pleasure escaped her lips when his cock was fully imbedded in her pussy once again.

"Because your body knows who the master is and the pleasure my hand can grant you."

His words taunted her but Emma clung to her pride. The battle was addictive in a way, some sort of test of her character. Julian wouldn't have her if she were weak, so Emma refused to yield to his demand.

"No."

Julian growled at her and suddenly pulled his cock free of her body. "Then you will not be granted release." His hand landed on her bottom several more times and she quivered with the pleasure that the blows sent through her pussy.

Emma gasped and her body trembled so violently she had to push back onto her knees to keep from falling to the ground. Her clit twisted in agony as the sting from Julian's discipline made her pussy even hotter. She looked up to see Julian's cock thrusting straight out of his open britches. She lifted a hand toward the swollen length and stroked her fingers over the spot under the head. Another growl shook Julian's chest as he watched her. Memory surfaced as she recalled exactly how Tellie had knelt before Herbert to suck his cock. Her pride demanded she reduce Julian to the same desperate state she was in. Rising up on her knees, she curled her fingers around his slick cock and opened her mouth to take the head between her lips. A harsh hiss was Julian's response as his hand cupped the back of her head, gently pressing her toward his cock.

"Suck my cock, Emma, make me your servant." Emma shivered as emotion joined the need clawing through her. No one had ever understood her so well. Julian was the only man who could master her body but it was a power she might wield over him in return. The fact that he knew that sent a wave of confidence through her. Emma relaxed her jaw and took more of his cock into her mouth. The scent of her own fluid joined the warm taste of his skin as she let her tongue flicker around the head of the cock in her mouth. She worked her fingers over the part that wasn't inside her mouth and enjoyed the rumble of enjoyment her actions drew from Julian. His hips were thrusting his cock toward her mouth with little jerks that he fought against, but his need for release drove him to surrender, too. She might be on her knees but Julian was captive to her control.

Julian suddenly caught her hair and pulled his cock out of her mouth. Emma raised her eyes to look at him and the flicker of admiration humbled her. It was more than lust, deeper than desire. Emma stared up at him and for the very first time understood what true passion was. It was this swirling combination of need and excitement. Passion was that uncontrollable force that flung you into an inferno of emotion-driven desire. The need to fuck was a primitive urge, buried inside every person, but passion was a unique reaction to that one person you might very well find yourself in love with.

Julian bent down and hauled Emma over his shoulder. He stood back up and heard her muffled giggles. His lips twisted into a grin because he was enjoying their games, both the sharp edge of need and the little tugs they both managed to get in on each other's tails. He had never teased a woman before or enjoyed one doing it to him. It was that very combination that made him even more determined to bind Emma to his life. It wasn't about marriage or any of the other words that society liked to invent to control sex. What burned in his soul was the need to touch her, smell her skin and know that she enjoyed his touch, in fact craved it as much as he did.

The door of the cottage shook violently as Julian kicked it closed with one boot heel. Emma held on to his wide back as he strolled into the room and dumped her onto the bed. Like many more practical homes, the bed was in the same room as the fireplace. Most families did not have coin for two fires and so they cooked and slept in the same room. The cottage was of good size and it smelled of a fresh cleaning. Julian's wool riding jacket dropped onto the bed frame corner post as Emma tried to get her legs untangled from her skirt. Julian watched her with his topaz eyes as his fingers made efficient work of the rest of his clothing. Emma was fascinated as he simply laid the garments aside and stood proudly before her in his natural form. There were not many people who had the confidence to shed their fashion so easily. Emma had never seen a man naked before and her eyes roamed over the muscles she'd felt and only caught glimpses of in a ruby haze.

His cock took her interest as her pussy cried out for more. Her clit was a dull ache now, the hunger never dying.

"I want to spill my seed inside you, Emma." The bed vibrated as Julian propped a hand on the mattress on either side of her body and leaned toward her. "Not in your mouth but deep inside that hot pussy. Would you like to know why? Because your body milked my cock last night. You didn't lie in bed out of some duty, you fucked me and came even harder when you felt my seed hitting your womb. Call it whatever pretty word you like, but your pussy milked my seed from my cock because you wanted me to mate you. Not any man, me." Julian kissed her hard and quick as Emma felt her blood race through her veins. She suddenly detested her dress and wanted to tear the cotton thing off her body like an angry tiger. Just taking it off wouldn't be enough, and Emma battled the urge to destroy the dress so that she might never have to suffer it binding her again. She broke the kiss as she struggled to undo the buttons that ran down the back of the bodice. Julian lifted her again and laid her facedown on the bed. Emma sighed as he began to free her from the dress. His blunt statement had her clit flickering with need again as her memory replayed exactly how it had felt to have his seed spurting up inside her pussy. The idea drew her into its shimmering light of remembered pleasure and Emma simply did not care what anyone might think except Julian.

A solid arm went around her waist as Julian pulled her off the bed and placed her on her feet. Her dress went up over her head, drawing her arms along with it, but Julian didn't pull the fabric free, he gave a twist and suddenly her arms were trapped in the little sleeves of her dress as Julian twisted the cotton into a knot behind her back. Her little thin corset was the only thing between her nipples and his eyes. A tug on the laces and the corset slipped down her body because Julian had even untied the shoulder straps. The position of her arms thrust her breasts up and forward as Julian cupped one in each hand.

"Stunning." His thumbs brushed her nipples, sending sensation down her body. The way he looked at her made her feel like the most beautiful woman on Earth. It was a surprising thought for Emma because she had spent so much of her life reminding herself to be practical. Beauty was often a shallow idea because it only referred to the current fashion. Next season that same feature might be the cause of ruin among the ton.

"You are such a splendid creature, Emma. Do you have any understanding what it is that pulls me to you? Drives me to abduction just to get between your thighs again?" Julian grinned slightly over his dramatic words as Emma felt her lips twitch up in response. Yes, he had abducted her and she secretly hoped Julian might do it again.

"I saw you face down my brother." Emma's face went white. Julian watched her eyes and there was no trace of fear in them, only surprise to hear he'd witnessed her stand against Herbert. "I enjoyed the fire burning in your belly that sent you there in defense of your family. It was stunning, did you know that? How deeply stirring I found your courage? It is your spirit that calls to me, Emma, so you may just compose another letter and a hundred more until you write one that does not place a barrier between us."

Temptation taunted her with the idea that Julian would be

around to read each and every one of those letters. Her heart swelled with the hope that their current addiction to each other would not fizzle out as quickly as it had erupted. Emma struggled against the bonds on her arms as she became too filled with emotion to stand still.

"Not yet, Emma. I have not yet heard you call me master. So, I must finish the task of taming you."

SEVEN

"REALLY, JULIAN." HER WORDS were husky and sounded as though they belonged to a stranger. Emma tried to smile at his game but her stomach twisted with anticipation as her clit burned for the challenge to begin.

"Really." Julian delivered that single word like a gavel hitting a desk. He leaned close enough for her to feel his breath on her moist lower lip. "Master."

Her arms were free a moment later as her dress was yanked free, but Julian scooped her body up and tossed her onto the bed. The bed ropes protested as Emma bounced in a tangle of limbs. She was bare except for her stockings and shoes and Julian caught one slim ankle and began to unbutton her shoe. It was the most awkward position; Emma was held by that solid grasp on her ankle with one leg raised up into the air and her pussy in plain view. Julian's eyes flickered over her body as he tossed her shoe across the room. He let her ankle go as he grabbed the opposite one and freed her shoe. He pulled her stockings off next but didn't drop them as Emma expected. A smirk covered his face a moment before he knotted one of the thin summer socks around her ankle and looped the other end around the headboard corner post.

"Julian!"

"Master!" Julian captured her free ankle and knotted the last stocking around it. He tied that one to the footboard post of the bed, spreading her legs across the length of the bed. Emma leaned back on her elbows as her pussy was placed on display. Julian didn't pull her bonds too tight and she was able to keep both legs bent at the knee with her feet resting on the surface of the bed, but she was spread wide with no way to close her legs. Julian smiled at his work and stroked a hand over her bare inner thigh. He took his time and then stroked the opposite thigh before looking back at her face.

"I enjoyed lapping at your clit." Her face instantly burned with a blush as Emma considered how much she was at his mercy. A crazy twist of excitement tore through her pussy at the idea of testing how far he might push her. While her body was bound, the key to release was in her grasp. One little word and she'd be free. That condition banished any trace of fear from her because it balanced the power between them.

Julian stroked a single finger over her open slit. He watched her face as his fingertip began at the opening of her pussy and then slipped up the wet center to her clit. Her hips jerked off the bed as he rubbed that little bundle of nerves.

"Such a responsive clit." Julian rubbed her clit a moment longer before slipping that finger down to her pussy entrance. "But this is tender as well." His finger thrust up inside her pussy as her body made a little wet sound.

"I have a confession for you, Emma." Julian worked that single finger in and out of her pussy with slow motion. Having had his cock thrusting inside her so recently, his finger wasn't nearly thick enough and her pussy ached to be stretched as it had been outside. "I'm hoping you take a very long time before calling me master."

Emma gasped at the look Julian aimed at her. His finger left her body and traveled up to her clit once again. Julian watched her eyes as he rubbed her clit just a bit faster than he had before. Heat bathed her skin like hot water as her bottom lifted from the bed to press harder against that single touch. A tiny whimper escaped her lips and Julian lifted his finger away from her spread body. He propped his hands on either side of her body as he leaned down and licked one of her nipples. Sensation shot down her body as Julian used only the tip of his tongue to circle the puckered tip. He finished the circle before sucking the entire nipple into his mouth. Emma fell back onto the bed as he flicked the tip of his tongue over the puckered nipple while he sucked on it. She jerked against her bonds as the head of his cock suddenly slipped up the center of her spread slit. Julian chuckled as he released her nipple and Emma looked down to see his hand wrapped around his cock. Julian moved his cock up the middle of her slit and then back down to the opening of her pussy. Her bottom gave a jerk as it lifted toward that hard cock, but all Emma gained was the tip pressing against her aching flesh.

Master. The word drifted through her brain as tempting as a hot bath on a cold night. All she need do was yield and Julian would fuck her hard, feed the hunger gnawing at her body. Julian chuckled and Emma realized he was watching her face, reading her emotions like printed text. He let his cock go and lowered his body between her spread thighs.

"Good girl, Emma. I expect more fight from you." And that idea excited him. Confidence built inside her as her mouth went dry. Julian used his fingers to pull the folds of her sex completely away from her clit before he leaned forward to lap the little bud. Her hips bucked as need twisted under his tongue. Emma clawed at the bedding as moans so primitive she didn't know she might make them escaped her throat. She was more like the mare just then, her body guiding her, not her brain. She had no care for the sounds, only the hot mouth sucking on her clit. Julian kept his laps slow and light. Climax remained out of reach as her hips strained toward his mouth.

"Please, Julian!"

Her plea was almost his undoing. Julian snarled between his clenched teeth as he looked at her pussy. The taste of her body filled his mouth as the scent of her musk invaded his brain. There was only one thing he craved at that time. To fuck. He needed to drive into her body and be as close to her as it was possible to get. He licked her slit instead and listened to her moan. It was a sweet sound because he'd wrung it from her. Making his way to her clit, Julian flicked his tongue over it as Emma thrashed against her bonds.

"Master." The word slipped from her lips without thought. Words had lost all meaning as her body heat rose to a level that made everything feel too hot. Sweat beaded on her skin as Julian gave a snort of pleasure and stood up. A moment later his cock thrust deeply into her pussy and Emma felt climax tear into her immediately. Her hips bucked toward Julian as he thrust quickly between her thighs. Her eyes flew open as Emma realized she needed his pleasure to mingle with hers.

"Come, Julian!" Her command hit his ears and he obeyed. His hands curled around her hips as he slammed his cock into her pussy. Emma cried out as her pussy contracted around his cock and she felt the hot spurt of his seed once again. It was a deeper satisfaction than she had ever known as her hips remained above the surface of the bed, pressing toward her mate as he held her in place for his seed.

Emma must have forgotten to breathe. Her head swam in a dizzy circle once the rush of pleasure released her. Her body collapsed to the bed as she panted and tried to calm her racing heart. Julian smoothed his hands over her body, rubbing the thighs that ached from her lifting toward him. He untied her ankles as he laid her out on the bed and then joined her. Once again Julian pressed her head down onto his chest and the sound of his heartbeat filled her head.

It was the most intimate embrace she had ever shared. Emma rested one hand on that hard chest as her fingers slid through the crisp hair that coated him. That only made him more male, the crisp hair opposed to her smooth skin. She didn't want them to be the same, it was their differences that fed her hunger. Her skin cooled as passion receded and Julian sighed before he sat up.

"I had better get you home before the gossips get to tearing too many holes in your reputation." Julian sounded angry but he stood up and picked up his britches. It would be so simple to just invite him back to the bed and forget the rest of the world. He tucked his cock into the front of the black riding pants and pushed the buttons through their holes. Emma felt her stomach twist as she watched the trappings of society going into place.

But a bubble of happiness surfaced as well. This private thing between them was theirs alone. It was their secret as well as haven away from the harsh realities that life often was. Between the dull and the mundane, there were moments like this when they might sneak away for the intimacy that transformed lust into love.

Julian pulled his shirt on next and frowned at her. "You had better marry me soon, Emma, or I don't think I will give much care to your reputation by the end of the week."

Emma gasped but a giggle ruined the stern sound as she watched Julian frown like a boy denied a freshly baked cake. He held up her dress and frowned even deeper.

"Have pity on me, Emma. Tell your father I'm madly in love with you and you fear for my sanity if we don't marry immediately."

"Maybe I fear for my own, Julian." The words rushed from her lips and Emma realized they were not born from silly jesting. She finally understood what all the poets were trying to convey in their works. Love truly was the most elusive of things but it was also irresistible. One tiny touch and your heart was enchained to another. Emma saw it burning in Julian's eyes, and his pride battled against its reality just as her own did. They might be the most frustrated lovers but they were also the most fortunate creatures on Earth to have found each other.

Julian caged her between his arms as he leaned over the bed again. His topaz eyes were unguarded as he looked into hers. He suddenly smiled at her and caught her mouth with a deep kiss. He pulled her off the bed and a sharp smack hit her bare bottom as her dress was dropped over her head. Emma struggled to raise her arms fast enough to get her hands into the sleeves of the garment.

"Hurry up, woman! You torment a poor man who is infected with love!" The dress fluttered into place and Emma looked up into Julian's eyes. They sparkled with humor as he turned her around. "Very unkind of you, Emma, letting me suffer this way."

Emma giggled because she just could not contain the sound. The shifting power between them was never going to stop amusing her. She peeked over her shoulder at Julian.

"The corset goes on first, Julian. I do hope you will make a better husband than maid."

A muffled curse escaped his lips as Julian began to undo the buttons he'd secured. He raised a dark eyebrow at her. "You will have to marry me to discover that."

EXHAUSTION WAS NIPPING AT her heels that night as Emma stood for Tellie to unfasten her dress. It was well into the early morning hours due to the entertainment her father was lavishing on his party guests.

Tonight, Emma found her blood racing with excitement as she enjoyed the whirl of the summer season. Love truly was worth longing for because now that it lived in her heart, contentment was not nearly enough.

The curtain that covered the exit to the servants' hallway swished aside and Tellie squealed as Julian walked straight into the room.

"Good Lord, woman, I'm going to marry your mistress tomorrow." Tellie turned to hide her grin but Emma caught the sly expression as she felt her own lips turning up in an identical one. Tellie really wasn't all that shocked, either, and Emma knew the truth of that matter!

The maid lifted the silk evening dress off her and took it to be hung up. Julian wiggled his eyebrows at her corset as Emma stifled a round of giggles. He turned and looked at the maid. "Good night."

Tellie cast another sly look at them both before she quit the room. Julian turned and caught Emma with one solid arm around her waist. "I thought that maid would never finish."

Julian's mouth landed on hers as Emma stretched up for her lover's kiss. The warm summer air stirred around them as they clung to each other. Emma broke the kiss as she backed out of his embrace and held out her hand.

"Will you be my lover tonight, Julian?"

He tilted his head to the side as his eyes moved down her frame. "Hmm, then tomorrow you will have to submit to your husband, now, won't you, Emma?"

Julian grasped her hand and stepped past her on the way to the bed. He pulled her with him and they landed among the turned-down bedding like two children. Excitement raced through her as Emma contemplated all the different forms their hunger might take. Tonight, they were lovers while tomorrow Julian might claim her as a prize. The friction their personalities produced was the real treasure of their love.

If fate were kind . . . it would never change.